"Do you even ha[...] fitted?"

"I have a limousine."

Lexi could see from the arrogant tilt of his head that his momentary panic was over and that he was firmly back in control. Which annoyed her. He'd almost seemed human earlier. Approachable.

"It doesn't seem that you've been worried about much at all where he's concerned," she said frostily.

His gaze sharpened. "Who do you think pays for this fancy establishment?"

"I meant emotionally. He needs something familiar. Do you have his favorite toy? Blanket?"

She raised her own chin challengingly. Mrs. Weston might have told her that he was some super-rich businessman, but he was clearly out of his depth in this situation.

"I have something better."

"What?"

"You."

From as far back as she can remember **MICHELLE CONDER** dreamed of being a writer. She penned the first chapter of a romance novel just out of high school, but it took much study, many (varied) jobs, one ultra-understanding husband and three very patient children before she finally sat down to turn that dream into a reality.

Michelle lives in Australia and when she isn't busy plotting, she loves to read, ride horses, travel and practice yoga.

Michelle Conder's first Harlequin Presents® title is now available in ebook!

3065—GIRL BEHIND THE SCANDALOUS REPUTATION
(Scandal in the Spotlight)

HIS LAST CHANCE AT REDEMPTION

MICHELLE CONDER

~ Dark, Demanding and Delicious ~

HARLEQUIN®
entertain, enrich, inspire™

Recycling programs
for this product may
not exist in your area.

ISBN-13: 978-0-373-52894-3

HIS LAST CHANCE AT REDEMPTION

Copyright © 2012 by Michelle Conder

HIS LAST CHANCE AT REDEMPTION

For Finn, Pia and Reif

CHAPTER ONE

COULD a man really die of boredom?

Leonid Aleksandrov stared down at his plate of—what had he ordered? Beef? Lamb?—and tried to blank out the blonde actress prattling away at him across the table as if he was one of her girlfriends.

To be fair it was most likely nervous chatter because, he had the good grace to acknowledge, he was a man on the edge. At the end of his tether, his executive assistant, Danny Butler, would say, and even a blind Russian boar could sense that.

But how could he be anything else? The tragedy that had occurred this week was newsworthy all over the world and the press were once again snapping at his heels to get a piece of him. Questioning who he was and sniffing into his past. Looking for Mafia connections one minute and then calling him a hero the next. But a true hero didn't have things in his life he regretted, did he?

Not that anyone would find anything on him. Seventeen years ago Leo had created a new identity for himself and thanks to Mother Russia being a country of smoke and mirrors he'd been able to bury the misery of his real childhood and reinvent a whole new one.

A much more palatable one.

So far no one knew any better. The press surmised that he was a dangerous man and, somewhat ironically, they didn't know the half of it.

But what on earth had possessed him—on his first day back in London—to take the latest 'it girl' to lunch at this high-end, nosey London eatery? On her birthday of all days.

Ah, yes, sex. Respite. A moment's relaxation. The gym had failed this week and he'd been looking for another outlet.

But no doubt Danny had thought no-frills sex in a hotel room was a bit cold-blooded on the actress's special day; hence the lunch date.

Leo shook his head. Danny had been with him for eight years now and even though he was as close to a friend as Leo had ever had, he was still a bit too modern and senti-mental for Leo's liking. And he'd blast him for suggesting the actress meet him in the hotel *restaurant* instead of the hotel *penthouse*.

What he had wanted was to get laid and get back to work, not sit down to a three course luncheon. Now, however, after forty minutes of polite chitchat about nothing more interest-ing than hairstyles and movie shoots, his libido had hit rock bottom.

Thank you, Danny boy.

'Leo, I swear, if I didn't know any better I'd think you hadn't listened to a word I've said.'

So not entirely without a brain then. That was something at least. A month ago they'd met at a party and she'd been texting on and off with innocent little invitations for Leo to attend this and that ever since. Well, 'this and that' was nigh and he couldn't have been less interested in taking things fur-ther if he was standing next to her wax look-alike at Madame Tussauds. In fact, right now, that would be preferable. Quieter, at least.

Leo pushed his half-eaten lunch aside and dropped his napkin onto his plate.

'Tiffany, it's been *enthralling*, but I have to go. Finish up. Have dessert—' he hesitated as he glanced at her emaciated figure '—or not.' He pushed back his chair and paused when he saw her overly plump bottom lip quiver; which may have been a trick of the light because a moment later her composure was flawless.

'Just like that?' She waved her hand insouciantly, her actor's face firmly in place. 'And to think people said you were dynamic. Fascinating. *Exciting*.'

Leo's eyes narrowed. 'We're in the wrong place for me to show you exciting, *dorogusha*, and now I'm all out of time.'

And interest.

'They also said you were heartless.' That last was delivered without even a hint of bitterness and his eyes narrowed on the challenging tilt of her head, his senses homing in on the purr in her voice.

So that was it. He was a challenge to her. A mountain she wanted to conquer. He could understand that even though he wasn't a man driven by challenges. He'd learned early on that rising to a challenge usually led to mistakes, pain. Leo didn't do that. He wanted something; he got it. No challenge required.

And Tiffany Tait had definitely overplayed her hand with that comment. Smarter women than her had tried to get their hooks into him without success. He was considered the consummate commitment-phobe and it was a reputation he had carefully cultivated for years.

He stood and buttoned his single-breasted suit jacket. '*They* are right. I am without a heart and no woman will ever change that. Something to remember next time you want to play games.'

With that he walked out. Leaving her and the Cartier bracelet Danny had kindly procured for her as a birthday gift at the last minute. No doubt Leo would hear about his unchivalrous behaviour in some gossip rag at some stage. Not that he cared. Today he'd been looking for a few moments of oblivion to push aside the memory of five of his men being bur-

ied alive in an accident on one of his construction sites, and
the agony of lifting mountains of cement and steel alongside
rescue crews all week to get to them.

They'd reached two in time; the other three were gone.
Just like his uncle seventeen years earlier.

Leo's mouth pulled tight as he wound his way through the
'beautiful people' who cast covert glances from behind their
crystal glasses.

Usually he loved his life. Proclaimed the richest man in
Russia, with enough super toys to fill any action flick, a sur-
feit of women clamouring to warm his bed and a business he
loved—he was understandably riding high. Today he'd almost welcome being back at the end of his father's belt than
return to work.

And really he shouldn't have been rude to Tiffany Tait. It
wasn't her fault she bored him. He chose that type of woman
for a reason—physical gratification and lack of emotional
connection. If he was getting bored with eye candy he'd just
have to get over himself.

Thirty minutes later and feeling marginally better now that
the restaurant ordeal was over he stalked through his outer
office and told his new secretary to get Danny—immediately.

Still nervous of him, she cleared her throat before speaking. 'He's already waiting for you, Mr Aleksandrov.'

'Leo,' he corrected her, pushing open his office door and
striding inside.

'If you ever send me to a poncy restaurant again instead of
a private suite when I tell you I want to get laid I'll fire you.'

'It's her birthday,' Danny replied smoothly.

Leo dropped into his leather-and-chrome chair and sur-
veyed the mountain of paperwork that had accumulated on
his desk in his absence.

'I don't care if it's her last day on earth. We both would
have had a better time in a bed. Send her another something

from somewhere, would you?' He picked up a stock market report and scowled. Bloody volatile fear-driven markets. When would people learn not to react to every flicker of the sun's rays as if it was about to go out?

'You were rude, then?'

Leo didn't look up. 'It's possible.'

He heard Danny sigh. 'I was about to call you back anyway. You have bigger problems to contend with right now.'

Leo went still at his EA's ominous tone. *Bohze*, not another site problem.

He didn't ask, just waited for Danny to continue. But instead of saying anything, Danny handed him a pink sheet of paper with tiny coloured flowers dotted along the top.

Leo read the brief message and his foul mood plummeted. 'You're not serious?'

'It seems so. I haven't been able to reach her by phone.'

'Have you had Security try to track her down?'

'They're on it but no luck so far. She says she's heading to Spain.'

'I can read.'

A heavy silence fell between them and Leo scanned the note once again to make sure he hadn't been mistaken.

Then he leaned back in his chair and rubbed the back of his neck, feeling his muscles bunch but not release. He crumpled the pink paper in his fist and lobbed it across the room. 'How many hours do we have?'

'Two. The childcare centre closes at five.'

Leo swore under his breath and jerked to his feet.

'It's only for the long weekend. She'll be back on Monday,' Danny added, highlighting the only positive in the message.

Leo stared out of his office window and watched the London Eye do a lazy circuit in the glittering summer sunshine. The wharf was a hive of teeming tourists probably spending more money than they had and he'd gladly hand over half of his vast fortune to any one of them if they could solve his current problem.

Four years ago he'd met a young model at Brussels Airport when all flights had been grounded due to inclement weather. Leo hadn't even thought twice about it. Beautiful, more-than-willing woman, long night. It made sense.

Her wanting to get pregnant to a rich stranger still didn't. The woman in question had been on the hunt for a rich husband instead of a rich career and had deliberately used a tampered condom. Three months later she'd come to him and told him the 'good' news.

She'd been hoping for a ring. What she'd got was a house and a monthly allowance once paternity had been confirmed.

Leo wasn't father material. He had blood running through his veins he had never intended to pass on. The fact that this model—Amanda Weston—had duped him had made him crazy. After the fog had cleared and logic had returned he'd done the honourable thing. He'd covered all her financial expenses and made her promise to keep the boy as far away from him as possible. He might have inadvertently given someone life but he wasn't about to completely stuff it up by being part of the child's life as well.

Recollections of his own childhood danced at the edges of his mind like circus performers wielding brightly coloured batons with which to prod him. First the death of three of his men had reminded him of the horrendous circumstances surrounding his beloved uncle's death and now the prospect of having to care for his three-year-old son was bringing up even worse memories. His mother. His father. His *brother*.

With ruthless determination Leo banished his memories and refocused on the one thing he could trust. Work.

He turned back to Danny. 'What's happening with the Thessaly ethanol plant?'

* * *

'So, you still haven't said. Are you going to Paris this weekend with Simon, or not?'

Lexi stopped trying to put the wheel back on a broken toy truck and looked over at her best friend and business partner, Aimee Madigan.

Aimee had one eye on the group of kids enjoying free play at the Little Angels childcare centre they had started together two years ago and the other on the yarn she was carefully winding back into a ball. 'And please don't tell me you have to work,' her friend added with a sense of resigned certainty.

Lexi grimaced. She was supposed to be heading to Paris for the long weekend with a guy she'd been seeing casually for two months. And no doubt Simon would expect their relationship to advance to the next stage—sex—but Lexi wasn't convinced that was such a good idea.

She had let herself be worn down by a man's pursuit once before and the experience still left a bitter taste in her mouth. Only she didn't really want to be worn down. The truth was, her life was wonderful as it was; she'd let herself be weakened once before by a man's pursuit and the experience still left a bitter taste in her mouth. 'You know the second centre is at a crucial stage of the planning. If I don't get the loan approved in the next week or so, we won't have one.'

'I take it things didn't go so well then with Darth Vader this morning?'

Lexi grinned at Aimee's use of the pet moniker they had attributed to their hard-nosed bank manager and tried not to feel despondent. 'He's still got some concerns about how much the renovations are costing and some aspects of the business plan.'

'I wish I could help you.'

Lexi shook her head. 'This is my area of the business and you do enough around here. I'll sort it somehow.'

Aimee stopped winding her wool and looked at Lexi as if she'd just had a great idea. 'I know, maybe you could do that somewhere between the Arc de Triomphe and the Louvre,' she suggested, only half tongue-in-cheek.

'Oh, yeah, I'm sure Simon would *really* love that!' Lexi laughed.

'Well, he *is* shelling out for The Ritz so it seems a shame to miss it altogether. And he does seem very nice.'

'He is,' Lexi replied, wishing Aimee would let the topic drop.

'Lex, you're still using work as an excuse to avoid having a proper relationship with a man,' Aimee reproved.

Lexi scraped her finger on the toy car. 'Ow, damn.' She sucked the scratch and tried to keep her answer light and simple. 'Maybe I just haven't met the love of my life yet.'

'And you won't with the amount of hours you spend here.'

'I'm happy.'

'Not every man is an immature skunk like Brandon, Lex, and it has been four years.'

Lexi pulled a face. She'd been best friends with Aimee since high school and she knew her friend had her best interests at heart. And she also knew Aimee was right, but Brandon's betrayal had echoed that of her father's just a little too closely and Lexi wasn't at all sure she was willing to risk her heart again any time soon.

'I know that,' she said on a sigh. And she did. But even thinking about having a relationship brought up all her old insecurities and the truth, which she was far too embarrassed to ever admit to anyone—including Aimee—was that she wasn't great at sex. Wasn't overly sexual at all. Which, if she was being completely honest, was the main reason she didn't want to go to Paris. That and the fact that she didn't actually *want* to have sex with Simon. But admitting that made her feel as if there was something wrong with her.

And maybe there was… Wasn't that what Brandon had implied?

She walked over to give the truck back to the three-year-old who had broken it. 'Here you go, Jake. Just be a bit more careful when you play with it this time.' She scanned the group and didn't even hear the high-pitched sounds of kids digging to China in the sandpit and chasing each other around the various climbing frames during their free play session. It was getting towards the end of the day and half the kids had already been collected. Her eyes fell on Ty Weston playing quietly by himself hammering at the small wooden table, and her heart gripped a little.

Professionally, Lexi would never admit to having a favourite at the centre, but personally she and Ty had clicked. Had done from the moment he'd joined the centre as a runty one-year-old. Small for his age back then, he was now veering on the taller end of the scale for three.

'You know,' Aimee began almost tentatively when Lexi picked up another tangled ball of wool and started winding it, 'we could always ditch the idea of the second childcare centre.'

'What?' Lexi was genuinely shocked by Aimee's suggestion. This was their dream and the area of London they were planning to open their new centre was in desperate need of decent childcare. 'I can't believe you would say that after all we've put into it. And I have no intention of quitting just because my love life is suffering and because we've had a few setbacks.'

'Lex, you *don't* have a love life and we're paying rent on an empty building that's nowhere near finished. Maybe you need to give up on the idea of us becoming the saviour of the childcare world.'

Fortunately for Aimee, Lexi didn't get a chance to respond to that because one of their co-workers interrupted them.

'Excuse me, Lexi.'

Lexi turned as Tina stepped through the double glass doorway leading into the main room.

'What is it, Tina?'

Tina grinned. 'There's a hot guy wanting to pick up Ty Weston but I don't know who he is.'

Hot guy? Probably a model, Lexi thought dismissively.

'His mother is supposed to be collecting him tonight,' Lexi said. But she wouldn't be surprised if the flaky Amanda Weston had forgotten. The woman didn't seem to care about her son and ever since her mother, Ty's grandmother and main carer, had passed away two weeks ago, Amanda had become even worse. 'What's his name?'

'Didn't say.' Tina waggled her eyebrows. 'But I think he might be a movie star.'

Lexi laughed at Tina's stage whisper.

'I'll be sure to get his autograph for you,' she whispered back.

'Forget the autograph. Just let him know I'm single.'

'How do you know *he* is?' Lexi countered.

Tina raised her left hand. 'No rings.'

'Maybe I should go,' Aimee interrupted gravely. 'This sounds serious.'

Lexi rolled her eyes and swiped her hands down her grubby peasant skirt. 'Yeah, I'm sure Todd would *love* that! Watch Ty for me, can you? He's been a bit fragile lately.'

She stepped inside the softly lit main room and noticed the outline of a tall, broad-shouldered man just visible through the window into her office. A sense of trepidation settled in her stomach at the very stillness he seemed to project through the glass.

Telling herself not to be dramatic, Lexi straightened her shoulders and opened the door to her office, stopping short when possibly the most divine-looking man she had ever seen turned to face her.

Hot guy?

The man was scorching. Tall and leanly muscled in a beautifully cut grey suit and black open-necked shirt. He had a chiselled jaw sporting a five o'clock shadow, heart-stopping blue eyes framed by jet-black lashes, close-cropped dirty blond hair and enough sexual confidence to make a courtesan blush.

Various film star names ran through her head but none of them seemed to match. No star she could recall had that air of controlled menace about them. Not that she'd met that many…or any, in fact. Her gaze rose back up over his superb physique and her breath stalled somewhere between her throat and her lungs as their eyes met. His gaze was that of a predatory animal sizing up its prey. Or maybe an army general contemplating war. Whoever he was, he was no ordinary movie star.

Lexi curved suddenly dry lips into a professional smile and ignored the way her stomach seemed to have bottomed out. 'Good afternoon. My name is Lexi Somers. How may I help you?'

Those dangerous blue eyes raked her from head to toe and made the strange feeling in the pit of her stomach slide lower.

'I'm here to collect Ty Weston.' His voice was dark, accented. Russian? Something East European anyway. Which explained the slashing cheekbones and strong jaw. Against her better judgement, she looked into his eyes again and was surprised not just because of her unexpected physical reaction, but because he also seemed familiar.

She had seen him before.

No. She shook her head and then masked the unconscious movement by stepping past him to the relative safety of the other side of her oak desk. She would definitely remember him if she'd seen him before. *And* his smell. Clean, citrusy with a hint of wood. She would *definitely* have remembered *that*.

Lexi thought about sitting down, but immediately discounted the idea. Even in her three-inch heels he towered over her and instinct warned her not to concede one of those inches to him or he'd steamroll right over top of her. She'd been cursing the shoes all day, having dressed formally for her meeting at the bank this morning and only realising she'd left her comfortable flats at home when she'd changed out of her business suit. Now she was glad for the extra height.

'And you are?' She kept her voice courteous, calling on years of defusing difficult situations in an attempt to lighten the tension in the room.

'Here to collect Ty Weston.' He looked down his slightly crooked nose at her and Lexi felt the first stirrings of irritation she usually had no trouble keeping in check.

'Yes. You said that. But I'll need a little more information before I can release him into your care.' Even saying that last word felt like a misnomer given his steely demeanour.

He folded his arms across his chest and the room seemed to shrink. 'What kind of information?'

'Your name for one.'

Despite her better judgement, Lexi dropped into her comfortable chair. Her feet were killing her and she hoped it would induce him to do the same; anything to make him seem a little less imposing. 'Please, take a seat,' she offered with forced equanimity.

He didn't answer, nor did he take up her suggestion. Just scanned the room like some sort of secret service operative and Lexi felt her pang of unease turn into a shiver of real dread. Should she be calling the police right now? Did the man have a gun thrust into the back of that expensive-looking suit?

Lexi gave herself a mental head slap. It wasn't like her to overdramatise situations. Still... 'I have to say you're making me feel distinctly nervous.'

His eyes found hers again and a jolt of something other than fear shimmied through her. 'I am Leo Aleksandrov.' His tone told her she should recognise who he was but she didn't. Her life was far too busy to read gossip magazines.

'I can tell that's supposed to mean something to me, but I'm sorry, it doesn't.'

He shrugged. His first human movement. 'That is of no consequence to me. Now, please—' he inclined his head in what Lexi imagined was supposed to be a demonstration of politeness but just came across as an incredibly superior gesture '—I am short on time.'

She frowned. 'What is your relationship to Ty Weston?'

'Not your concern,' he said, his nostrils flaring slightly as if the question was beneath him.

'Actually, it's very much my concern—' Lexi barely controlled her growing annoyance '—if you're serious about taking him with you.'

'Did I not say I was short on time?'

Lexi's eyebrows hit her hairline at his condescending tone. Just who did this guy think he was? 'And did I not say I required more information from you? We don't usually allow the children in our care to just go off with anyone who happens in off the street. There are procedures to follow. Forms to sign.'

He looked as if he hadn't considered that. Then his eyes raked over her again and Lexi wished she was still wearing her professional suit from earlier. 'I'd like to speak to the manager.'

She smiled, never more pleased at being able to utter her next words. 'I am the manager.'

He stared at her and Lexi couldn't drag her eyes from his intense blue eyes.

'I apologise,' he said finally, a mocking lilt in his voice that suggested otherwise. 'It seems we are at loggerheads, Ms Somers—'

'Miss.'

Now why had she said that? She preferred Ms!

'*Miss* Somers,' he intoned. 'And while I appreciate your concern for Ty Weston's welfare, I have permission from the boy's mother to collect him this evening as she is apparently out of town.'

Lexi frowned at his use of the word 'apparently.' 'I'm sorry, but it doesn't seem as if she has informed the centre of this change. Do you have proof of this permission?'

He paused and his mouth quirked slightly upwards. 'Alas, I left it back in my office.'

Lexi nodded, not at all convinced by what he was saying.

'Well, alas, Mr—' Damn, what was his last name again? '—you'll just have to come back when you have your proof.' She stood up. 'Now, if you'll excuse me—'

'You're dismissing me!' The shocked outrage on his ruggedly handsome face would have made her laugh any other time but right now butterflies were tap dancing in her stomach and making her feel strange.

'Yes, I do believe I am.'

He planted his hands on top of the paperwork on her desk and leaned towards her. 'Listen, Miss Somers, I've had just about as much as I can take of your obstinacy.'

'*My* obstinacy?' Lexi leaned back in her chair and tried to stare him down. Which wasn't easy. In his anger his eyes had taken on a cold precision that could cut through lead. 'That's rich.'

Maybe she *should* call the police.

Some of her nervousness must have shown because his eyes narrowed. 'I can assure you this is all completely aboveboard.'

'Then you won't mind if I contact Amanda.'

He straightened up and pulled at his cuffs. 'Please do. And if you get through pass the phone this way.'

Frowning even harder Lexi collected Ty's file from the corner cabinet, conscious of his eyes on her the whole time. Ignoring him she returned to her seat and dialled Amanda Weston's mobile number.

After a minute the phone clicked over onto voicemail and Lexi left a brief message asking her to call and hung up.

'She's not available,' she said a little unnecessarily, given he had heard her message.

The man, Leo Alek-someone, didn't seem surprised.

Just then another parent arrived at the gate to be buzzed into the centre and Lexi rose to her feet. 'If you'll excuse me, I need to attend to someone else and while I do I'll double check with my colleagues as to whether Amanda passed on a message about you.'

She headed towards the door and felt his body move infinitesimally, as if he planned to follow her.

'I wouldn't,' she warned him coolly, heart pounding a mile a minute. 'We have panic buttons carefully placed throughout the centre and if you follow me I'll set one off.'

He stared at her for a long moment and then smiled.

Lexi's breath caught at the dazzling effect of that smile. Then it turned lazy as he noted her reaction. 'You're bluffing, Miss Somers.'

Yes, she was. They had one panic button in the centre and she had no doubt he'd be on her before she could even instruct someone to activate it.

'Follow me and find out,' she dared, wondering at the husky challenge in her voice. Something about this man's inherent sense of authority, that came with being super rich, or super famous, rubbed her up the wrong way.

He cocked his head, his eyes running over her as if she was a delicacy he wouldn't mind nibbling. Heat constricted her throat and when his gaze dropped to her chest her breasts seemed to expand and tighten in a completely visceral response that was as shocking as it was unexpected.

His eyes, no longer icy, met hers and lust, the like she had never experienced before, exploded deep in her belly as she registered the inherent interest he didn't have the good manners to hide. 'Don't be long.'

Don't be... Lexi stalked out of the room.

Had she ever met a ruder, more charismatic man in her life?

CHAPTER TWO

LEO watched the petite brunette sweep out of her office as if the hounds of hell were after her, her ponytail bobbing behind her head like an overwound pendulum.

Run, angel, run.

He smiled to himself, unable to take his eyes off her trim figure.

He shouldn't have goaded her like that but he couldn't resist the way her exotic golden eyes had sparkled at him crossly and the way her creamy skin had flushed pink.

She'd had the strangest effect on him the minute she'd come striding through the door like some field marshal about to do battle. Her heart-shaped face tipped at an angle that said she could easily take on Alexander the Great and win.

Okay, maybe it wasn't the *strangest* effect. Maybe it was a purely sexual one, but it had hit him from left field because she wasn't his usual type. Too uptight—despite the Snow White attire—and too small. Delicate even. Her waist appearing so slender he could wrap his hands around her without any trouble at all. He liked his women a little taller, a little more sophisticated and a *lot* more accommodating.

He cupped his hands behind his head and spied the contents of her desk. Papers, brightly coloured pens, cotton dolls and a computer keyboard, all neatly arranged. Soft pink curtains hung from the single window and various child related paraphernalia lined the walls.

And some New-Agey smell had got up his nose and he had yet to locate the source. He wondered how Lexi Somers smelled and whether her neat figure would live up to the promise outlined in her prim blouse and red skirt. Then he told himself to quit it—he wasn't here for that.

Only his mind had already conjured up a pleasurable image of the hint of puckered nipples beneath the lacy bra she wore and his mouth watered as he wondered at their colour. Their taste. He'd noticed her response to his perusal of her body earlier and as much as she might be trying to appear cool and calm—he could tell she was a fireball of nerves inside.

What would she be like in bed? Coolly efficient, or hot and abandoned?

The thought hadn't fully formed in his mind before the annoying bell over her office door tinkled. His senses stood to attention at the sound of her determined footsteps crossing the linoleum flooring in shoes more befitting a party-girl than a childcare manager. And what was up with that? Clearly she was a woman who played on her sexuality.

Definitely hot and abandoned, he decided, and unconsciously breathed deep as she skirted past him. Just the hint of vanilla and…musk? Seductive, whatever it was, he thought, slightly bemused at his one-track mind.

'I'm sorry you've wasted your time, Mr…'

'Aleksandrov.' He said his surname more slowly, amused despite himself that she might really not know who he was. It happened so rarely nowadays.

'Aleksandrov.' She smiled, her hands folded primly together on her desk as if the matter was resolved.

Leo twisted his mouth into a smile and slouched back in the wooden chair built for a doll. 'And why is that, *Miss* Somers?' he asked casually, unwilling to refute her mistaken belief that she was in control of this situation just yet.

'I've checked with my colleagues and there has been no message about a change in pick up arrangements so I cannot release Ty Weston into your care.'

Leo felt an itch attack his left eyebrow and ignored it. Just as he ignored her statement. Instead he folded his arms across his chest and stared her down, waiting for her to break. Surprisingly, she held his gaze longer than he had expected. Then she sat straighter. 'I think it's time you left.'

If only he could.

'What are you going to do when nobody comes to collect Ty?'

A flicker of doubt clouded her eyes and she let out a pent-up breath. 'Look, I've had a lousy day so far and you're not making it any better. I have no idea who you— Oh! You're—'

'Ty's father.'

He spoke at the same time as she had deduced the information and he raised a mocking brow at her cleverness.

'The eyes. You have his eyes.'

Leo didn't know that. He'd never once looked at the photos his security team provided in their regular updates on his son.

A sheen of sweat broke out across his brow at the thought of meeting him now. Already emotions and guilt he'd had no trouble keeping at bay for years were swelling inside him like heavy rain filling a river, and he mentally cursed Amanda Weston and her conniving ways.

Leo stood up, ignoring the heat of Lexi Somers' gaze as it raked over his chest, pulling his stomach muscles tight.

Perhaps he should have told her his relationship to Ty from the outset, but the last thing he wanted was word to get out that he had a son. If it did he'd have to supply Ty with a security detail for the rest of his childhood and he had wanted to avoid that at all costs. 'Fine. Now you can go get him. I'll wait here.'

The surprise that had softened her full lips disappeared and she shook her head. 'I'm sorry; I can't do that.'

Leo felt the return of his earlier annoyance at her stubbornness. 'Why not?'

'You're not on his list of appointed people permitted to collect him.'

Chort vozmi! 'What a load of rubbish,' he rasped.

She stood up to face him and gripped the edges of her desk. 'It's not rubbish. We have procedures in the centre to ensure the children's safety and—'

'If you knew who I was you wouldn't be arguing with me.'

He blew out a breath. He sounded like a self-important ass and the look on the brunette's face said she'd come to the same conclusion.

'Why? Because you're above the law?' The imperious question didn't require an answer but he wanted to give her one. He wanted to take the line his Cossack ancestors would have done: press her up against the wall and take what her wide-spaced golden eyes had been offering since she'd first marched into the room. Then he'd take his son and get the hell out of there.

Pity a couple of centuries had spoiled that option.

'I'm his father,' he ground out, the words sounding strange to his ears.

'A father whose name is not on any of our forms,' she reminded him. 'And why is that?'

Leo reined in surging guilt that threatened to spiral into rage and paced two steps to the back of the room.

He sucked in a deep breath, knowing that logically she had a point even though her question was way out of line.

He turned back to face her. 'Look, Miss Somers—' he unclenched his jaw '—I want to be here about as much as you want me here but I don't have a choice. Amanda delivered a note to my office advising me that there was no one else to take care of Ty. Otherwise I wouldn't be here.'

'Are you having custody issues?'

Leo felt his eyes harden. 'I am not about to discuss my personal business with you.'

She stood firm. 'And I'm not about to release a child into the care of a man I've never met before and who is not on his list of trusted carers.'

Leo rubbed his neck. 'Try his mother again.'

She looked as if she wouldn't but then picked up the phone and hit redial.

'Still no answer.'

Leo swore and saw her eyes widen in silent reprimand. Too bad. The angel didn't like his language.

Then he returned to the doll's chair and sprawled in front of her. 'So what do we do now?'

For the first time since she returned she looked unsure and swivelled around to check the clock behind her.

'Half an hour to go, angel. Maybe we should find something else to do other than argue to make the time go quicker.'

Her eyes took on the size of the dinner plates his lunch had been served on and he cursed his rampaging libido. What was he doing thinking about sex with this woman at a time like this? 'Forget I said that.'

'I most certainly will. It was tacky in the extreme.'

Leo's eyes wandered over her with insolent abandon. 'Don't pretend you haven't thought about it, angel.'

She gasped and he smiled at her outrage. 'I most certainly have not! And do not call me angel.'

He smiled. She had. And so had he.

'I'll call you whatever I want and you're a liar.'

'And you're incredibly rude.'

He shrugged and checked the clock. 'Are you seriously going to make me wait until six o'clock before I can take him?' He'd never come up against such resistance from a woman before.

'No. I'm going to call the police.' She reached for the phone and he leaned across the desk and covered her hand with one of his. Sensation shot up his arm at the contact and for a moment all he could do was stare at her.

Time seemed suspended between them and then she wrenched her hand out from under his. 'Get your hands off me.'

'Settle down, Miss Somers, before you get hysterical.'

'I do not get *hysterical*. But you are crossing the line Mr Aleksandrov, and I want you to leave.'

Leo scrubbed his face. At least she remembered his name this time. 'I apologise. Call the police if it makes you feel better but it won't change anything. Amanda Weston has done a runner for the weekend and I'm all the kid's got.'

The angel rubbed the back of her hand as if she could still feel his touch and Leo's fingers flexed involuntarily because he could definitely still feel the silk of her skin. 'That remains to be seen.'

He glanced at the clock. 'Five minutes to go. Surely Amanda would be here by now if she was coming.'

'Not necessarily. She's often late, sometimes even forgetting to turn up at all.'

'What?' He was genuinely shocked by her comment and he saw the moment she knew she'd said too much. 'How many times?'

'Pardon?'

'How many times has she forgotten?'

'I can't remember.' She tucked a strand of hair behind her ear and he knew she was lying. He stared at her until she grew uncomfortable. 'A few since her mother passed away.'

He frowned. 'Her mother died?'

'She fell and broke her hip two weeks ago. I understand there was a complication with the surgery.'

He shook his head. 'I didn't know.'

'Why am I not surprised.'

It was a statement, not a question, and he scowled, deciding to ignore her disparaging tone. 'Why should that affect when Amanda picks the boy up?'

'Because she doesn't normally do it. As I understand it her mother was Ty's main carer.'

Leo frowned. Ty's grandmother had taken care of him? Maybe he should have read those reports after all.

'You didn't know that either, did you?' The angel didn't look impressed and he wanted to tell her she had no right to judge him.

'So it would seem,' he snapped, getting up and stalking the short distance to the rear of the room and back.

Leo noticed that she watched him as if she was trying to read him and he felt uncomfortable under her close scrutiny. He instinctively knew that if he told her he'd never even met his son she'd take umbrage and probably call in the army to deal with him and the truth was—he was a little worried. Danny was organising a nanny to meet him at his apartment to take over from him but...what would he do with a three-year-old until then?

Long suppressed memories of his baby brother spiked in his head—that soft little body, his cheeky grin, the way he had called him 'Layo.' Leo swallowed past the bile in his throat and refixed his gaze on Lexi Somers. His eyes dropped to the row of pearl buttons on her blouse and he imagined grabbing the collar and ripping them off. Imagined baring her to his hungry gaze and lifting her onto the desk and burying himself deep inside her. His body hardened, but sex wouldn't change the inevitable, only delay it, and he knew that was the reason it was on his mind so much since he'd arrived here. He was trying to distract himself. It had nothing to do with the brunette with the tiny waist and golden eyes.

'Mr Aleksandrov, are you okay?' He blanked his expression and told himself to stop being an ass and figure out this problem. Give him a stock market crash or a potential hotel site to assess and he'd have the situation under control in minutes. Dealing with the needs of a young child was so far removed from his reality he was struggling to be one step ahead of the issues.

Then it hit him. He'd forgotten to treat this situation like a business transaction. And hadn't he learned that everything came down to one thing?

'How much do you need to hand Ty over?'

'Excuse me?'

His eyes grew flinty. 'You heard. I'm a wealthy man.' He raked her with cool eyes. 'I'm sure your wardrobe could do with an update.'

Her mouth fell open and she stared at him as if he'd just asked her how to build a pipe bomb. 'Are you seriously trying to bribe me?'

Leo closed his eyes and then glanced at the ceiling before bringing his gaze back to her. He stood up. 'I already told you I'm short on time and you've wasted enough of it. I'm the boy's father; even you recognised that, so just—'

The phone ringing interrupted him and they both stared at it as if it were a snake. Then the angel leaned over to pick it up. He could tell straight away it was Amanda by the way her eyes flew to his. 'I see,' she murmured, before turning her back on him.

Leo's anger spiked and he lunged for the phone and yanked it out of her hands. 'Amanda, what do you—' *think you're doing?* he finished silently as the call was disconnected. He stared at the phone and swore viciously before tossing it onto Ty's file.

He felt confined and edgy in the tiny room. Then the annoying tinkle above the door sounded and a blonde poked her head through and eyed him as one would a dangerous animal. Which was exactly how he felt.

'Everything okay in here, Lex?'

Lexi's eyes flashed to his and he waited for her to say no.

'I think so. But can you hang around for another couple of minutes?'

'Sure. Ty is the only one left and Tina's gone.' The woman glanced in his direction and then dropped her eyes.

'Okay. I'll have this sorted in a jiffy,' Lexi said.

Leo looked at her. 'What's a jiffy?'

She seemed momentarily confused and then shook her head. 'I have no idea. It's a figure of speech. You're Russian?'

'*Da*. Yes. And you are English?'

'Yes.'

Something indefinable passed between them and then, thankfully, she shook her head and broke the connection. 'Okay. It seems that Amanda *has* gone away for the weekend and she just had enough time to tell me that you are Ty's father before you wrenched the phone from my hand like a Neanderthal.'

Leo didn't flinch at the criticism. 'Good. Then I can go.'

He stood and heard her release a noisy breath before she too rose to her feet.

'What now?' he growled, desperate to put this woman with her accusing golden-green eyes behind him.

'Why are you not on any of his forms?'

'Amanda has sole custody.'

'Why?'

'At the risk of sounding rude, Miss Somers, that's none of your business.'

'You're wrong.' She rounded her desk and stood in front of him. 'Ty is in my care and as I don't have written authority to hand him over to you I could still lose my licence as a childcare provider if I released him to you and something happened to him.'

'I appreciate your predicament but that is not my fault. Amanda should have made the proper arrangements.'

She considered him for a moment. 'Promise me you're not

some maniac of a father who is going to do something terrible the moment you have him alone.'

The skin on Leo's face pulled tight and his mouth went dry as she inadvertently tore a strip off one of the bandages concealing his childhood wounds. He was aware that his breathing had become shallow and that his blood was roaring in his ears.

He couldn't seem to tear his eyes away from hers and yet looking into her innocently questioning gaze was searing him with pain. 'I would never intentionally hurt my son,' he said hoarsely, his accent thicker as he fought to contain memories from the past.

He waited for her to contradict him. To say that she could see the blackness inside him, but she didn't. Instead she nodded curtly. 'Follow me.'

He released a harsh breath and followed her out into the main area of the centre, which was eerily neat and quiet. The blonde from before stepped through the opposite doorway. 'Ty is in the sandpit.'

'Thanks, Aimee. You go ahead. I'll be home shortly.'

'I'll probably be at Todd's.'

Lexi smiled and Leo's stomach did a somersault. 'I'll see you next week then.'

'Have a fun time away if you decide to go.' She raised her eyebrows and Leo wondered where Lexi Somers was going this weekend and why he cared. Then he forgot about it as the blonde walked away and he was confronted with an empty doorway.

His heart felt like a dead weight in his chest as he stepped through it and gazed at the blond-haired toddler happily making truck sounds as he scooped sand into the digger.

Chort vozmi. God damn it. He couldn't do this.

He turned to the woman behind him and gripped her arms as a fear he hadn't felt in years assailed him.

* * *

'You can't do what?' Lexi asked, her eyes racing across Leo Aleksandrov's suddenly pale face. He looked as if he were facing a smoking gun and she had no idea what to do. Her heart hammered in her chest. This close, she could see the blue of his eyes was shot through with silver and the stubble lining his jaw made his face impossibly handsome. 'Mr Aleksandrov?'

Her soft tone seemed to bring his eyes back into focus because he let her go and stepped backwards as he turned to stare at his son.

She rubbed her arms and glanced at Ty, who was regarding them curiously, no hint of recognition on his face at all. She tried to remember what Amanda Weston had said about Ty's father when she had first enrolled Ty at the centre but her memory was hazy. Something about him not being interested in Ty and a request that they not ask Ty about him. Obviously, whatever had happened between Amanda and Leo, it had not ended well and Ty had borne the brunt of that.

Lexi felt sick. She hated men who didn't take responsibility for their actions, who didn't care enough about their children to spend time with them.

Trying to quell her rising anger for Ty's sake, Lexi stepped forward. 'Ty, come on. Your da— Oh!'

Strong fingers bit into her upper arms as the man behind her grabbed her and hauled her back against him. Lexi stumbled in her high heels and fell back against a chest as rock-solid as granite. The breath left her lungs as one of his powerful arms banded her torso just below her breasts to keep her upright.

She instantly caught fire at his touch, unbidden lust tightening her breasts and sending a spiral of heat straight to her pelvis. Shocked by her instant sexual response—a response she'd been trying to deny since she'd first seen him—Lexi turned in the circle of his arms with every intention of pushing him away. Only once her hands flattened against the brick wall of his chest, his heat and his scent had a paralysing effect on her senses. Now she didn't want to push him away. Now she wanted to rise up onto her toes and kiss him. As if reading her thoughts, his eyes darkened to navy and took on a fierce quality that sent her senses into overdrive.

The faint buzzing of the airconditioning and the gentle sound of the wind chimes receded and Lexi was completely captivated as his head slowly lowered to hers. His hands at her waist tightened, pulling her inexorably closer, and her startled gaze flew to his as she felt the unmistakable edge of his erection brush against her belly.

His eyes held hers, his mouth hovering just out of reach, their breaths mingling, and Lexi couldn't move. Then his gaze clouded over, registering the shock she felt, and before she could suck in another breath he shoved her back from him and stalked inside.

Lexi followed him to the doorway as if in a daze, her body sending all sorts of mixed messages to her brain. One of which was to follow him inside and press herself up against him and never let go. Which was just crazy! She never behaved like that. Not even with Brandon!

'He doesn't know I'm his father.'

The harsh words broke into her personal thoughts and when she realised what he had said she couldn't hide her horror. 'How—'

'We've never met.'

What?

Lexi gripped the door frame, shaking her head. 'That's not possible.'

Leo's face as he looked at her was grim, all signs of his earlier arousal gone, while her own body still felt soft and jittery from the shock of all that maleness pressed so intimately against her own. She'd been right in her premonition before. The man was lethal—just not in the way she had expected.

His mouth tightened and she realised she was staring at it,

wondering how it would have felt if he hadn't stopped himself before. If she'd taken matters into her own hands and... *whoa, girl, hold the fort. You do* not *want to kiss this man.*

'I assure you it is,' he rasped raggedly.

Lexi's mind retraced their conversation and a thousand questions winged into it. But uppermost in her thinking was Ty's welfare. He hadn't been the same since his grandmother had passed away and now, to be taken by a strange man for three days—even if he was his father—could have a huge psychological impact on him.

And could she trust that this dangerous Russian was telling the truth about why he wanted Ty?

She forced herself to meet Leo's guarded eyes and willed her mind to concentrate on what was important. 'If that's true, he's not going to feel comfortable going with you,' she informed him shortly.

He rubbed the back of his neck and glanced away. 'I know. I should have thought of that earlier and organised the nanny to meet me here instead of my apartment.'

'Nanny?' Lexi frowned and glanced behind her to make sure Ty was still playing happily. 'Has Ty met this person before?'

'No.'

'Then he won't be happy with her either.'

'She'll know what to do.'

'Not necessarily. Do you even have a proper car seat fitted?'

'I have a limousine.'

'That doesn't answer my question. Listen, if Ty doesn't know you and you're taking him to an unfamiliar place, that will be scary for a three-year-old. Not to mention potentially damaging to his psyche.'

'You let me worry about his psyche,' he growled impatiently and Lexi could see from the arrogant tilt of his head that his momentary panic from before was over and that he was firmly back in control.

'It doesn't seem that you've been worried about much at all where your son is concerned,' she said tartly.

His gaze sharpened. 'Who do you think pays for this fancy establishment?'

'I meant emotionally.'

He looked at her as if she were speaking a foreign language and she huffed out a breath. Arguing was not going to solve this situation. 'He needs something familiar. Do you have his favourite toy? Blanket?'

For a minute he looked utterly lost and despite the fact that she despised his type, her heart went out to him.

He paced away from her and it seemed an age before he answered. Then he turned and her breath stalled at the sight of the bold smile that tilted the corners of his sexy mouth. 'I have something better.'

She was almost afraid to ask. 'Like what?'

'Like you.'

CHAPTER THREE

'WHY is he crying?' Leo asked, tugging loose another button on his shirt, which felt suddenly too tight. Ty had been crying on and off for half an hour and the sobs were twisting his gut to the point where he couldn't concentrate on work.

Lexi Somers, who had reluctantly accompanied him to his apartment two hours ago, reached across and took the distressed toddler from the matronly arms of the nanny, Mrs Parsons, whom Danny had organised. Instantly the boy cuddled into her and started sucking his thumb, huge teardrops clinging to his lower lashes.

Leo was aware that his pulse was racing just looking at his son and turned his attention to the woman holding him. Which wasn't much better because his mind instantly recalled the feel of her soft body against his and the moment he'd almost kissed her. As if he needed that complication right now. Today, at lunchtime, he would have welcomed the way she made him feel. Now, with his world unravelling at the seams, the last thing he needed to think about was sex. Especially sex with a cute woman who was utterly furious with him.

'He's not comfortable with Mrs Parsons yet, but that's to be expected,' she answered him briskly, one of her hands rubbing Ty's back soothingly. 'This is all very traumatic for him.' The reproach in her voice was unmistakable.

Not just for him, Leo thought.

'He seems very comfortable with you,' he said.

'I've looked after him almost every weekday for two years. It's only natural he feels comfortable with me.'

Leo felt movement behind him and turned to see Danny standing in the door of his home office. 'Dmitri is on the phone.'

'Right.' Due to the delay in collecting Ty, Leo still had work to wrap up. But first he needed to sort the problem of Ty and the nanny. 'You take him to bed,' he instructed Lexi. 'And then—'

'Please.'

Leo blinked at her quiet reprimand.

He thought about telling her that if she interrupted him one more time with that gorgeous mouth he'd do something they'd both regret but found himself in the unique position of needing somebody else more than they needed him. A situation he did not like at all. He had to get rid of her and the sooner the better. 'Please, Miss Somers, would you be so kind as to take my son to his bed?'

He could tell she wasn't fooled by his mocking tone, but that was okay. He knew she'd do it. Ever since she had told Ty that this 'nice' man was taking them on an adventure and had made it sound as if it could rival Disney World he knew she was a soft touch under her no-nonsense exterior—a weakness he was ruthless enough to exploit.

'Which room is his?' she muttered.

'This way.' Leo hadn't thought about which of his spare rooms to give Ty, but they were both the same so he chose the first one he came to.

He opened the door and inhaled vanilla as Lexi moved past him and looked around the room, a frown marring her smooth forehead.

King-sized bed, bedside tables, French windows leading

to an outside balcony, private bathroom. What was there to frown about? Except maybe the absence of a cot. *Chort vozmi.* He hadn't thought of that.

'Are they locked?' She nodded towards the French windows and spoke softly as the toddler was almost asleep in her arms, something Leo was glad about because he couldn't look at Ty without remembering his brother, Sasha.

'Of course,' he said, but he walked over and rattled the handles anyway.

'He really has never been here before has he?' she said, almost to herself.

'I told you that.'

'Yes, but I don't think I wanted to believe you.'

'I don't lie.'

She cast him a fathomless look. 'Can I have some more pillows?'

'Why?'

'Because he'll feel more secure if he's surrounded by pillows. This bed is too big for him.'

Leo opened the inbuilt wardrobe and pulled out three spare pillows and placed them on the end of the bed. 'Anything else?'

'Pyjamas.'

He glanced at Ty's jeans and T-shirt. 'Can't he sleep in what he's got on?'

'Do you sleep in jeans?'

Her sharp rebuke both surprised and irritated him.

'Are you trying to find out what I sleep in, Miss Somers?' he asked, wondering if her eyes flashed golden when she was aroused as they did when she was angered.

He expected her to snap at him but instead she smiled sweetly. 'I already know. It's called a coffin.'

Leo blinked, astounded at her unexpected sassiness and then she surprised him again by shushing him. 'Just go.' She waved him away with her free hand as if he were an annoying insect. 'I'll take care of this.'

Leo left, not sure whether to be bemused or outraged at her temerity.

Lexi fixed the bed so that Ty wouldn't fall out of it and then sat beside him while he fell into a deep sleep.

Then she picked up her phone and called Aimee in case she hadn't left for her boyfriend's house and was worried as to why she hadn't returned to their shared apartment. When Lexi told her who Ty's father was she could almost see Aimee slap her forehead.

'I knew I recognised him. Oh, my God. I didn't know he had a son.'

'What do you know about him?' Lexi found herself asking without actually meaning to. Because really she already knew any information Aimee could impart would just be more nails in the coffin she had accused him of sleeping in. Her lips twitched now at the remembered surprise on his face when she'd said that. Clearly people didn't tell him when he was being overbearing and arrogant often enough.

'He's mega wealthy. And I mean *mega*.' Aimee added with emphasis. 'Russian. Has been in the papers all week because he helped rescue two of his workers from a massive construction accident in Dubai. Remember, I told you about it.'

'Mmm,' Lexi said noncommittally. She had a vague recollection but the problems with their second centre had been taking up a lot of her head space lately.

'He also changes his girlfriends as often as he changes his underwear and is supposed to be fantastic in bed. *Hubba hubba*.'

'And which magazine did that little titbit come out of?' Lexi asked, thinking that it was most likely true.

'I can't remember. Anyway, what's he like?'

'Arrogant, rude, obnoxious.' Chiselled, gorgeous and utterly male, a little voice taunted.

Which she promptly ignored. She'd met Leo Aleksandrov's type before. Oh, not with the mega-wealthy tag, but arrogant men who viewed permanent relationships the way they viewed dental hygiene—sometimes required, but not necessarily so.

Her father had been one of those: a professional golfer who had never married her mother despite having two children with her, and who had then left them all to take up with his mistress. And Brandon had been no better. At the time they'd met he'd been a charismatic, well-connected university jock who had pursued her and convinced her he was falling for her, all in the name of sport.

Finding out that she had been played like so many other girls he had gone after had made her feel ill, as had his complaint that she had not only been too serious, but that she had been below average in bed. Of course she hadn't *believed* him, but it hadn't stopped her confidence from taking a heavy knock. So heavy, in fact, she hadn't dated seriously since.

Suddenly an image of Simon popped into her mind and she groaned. She couldn't do it. She wasn't ready to get serious with anyone yet. Maybe she never would be and that might not be a bad thing. She had good friends, a growing business...

Lexi realised Aimee was still talking about Leo and felt rude for being so caught up in her own thoughts she hadn't been paying attention. 'I'm sorry, Aim, I haven't been listening but I don't want to talk about this man any more. He's too irritating for words.'

'Irritating or irresistible?' her friend joked.

'I'm not going to dignify that with an answer,' she said, ignoring her brain's contradictory messages about him. 'But don't tell anyone about Ty being his son. I'm not sure what's going on yet, but I would hate Ty to get hurt in any way.'

She rang off and let herself out of the room, leaving the bedroom door slightly ajar in order to listen out for Ty.

She walked down the wide carpeted hallway, taking in the astounding dimensions of the sleekly designed penthouse apartment she was in. So this was how the other half lived!

It was like being in another world. The whole apartment looked as if it had come straight out of some modern architecture magazine, with not a rumpled doily in sight. She smirked as she thought about what Leo Aleksandrov would make of her and Aimee's shabby little two-room apartment, with throw rugs and papers and half completed sewing projects hanging around on the dining room table. If she were to put down anything half completed here it would likely get up and run away. And while the place was undoubtedly beautiful, it lacked soul. It lacked that special quality that made a house a home.

Not that it mattered, she thought, as she stopped in the doorway of the main sitting room, when the exterior walls were made up almost entirely of glass and showcased a view of London Lexi would normally have to buy a ticket to see.

And in front of that impressive wall of glass was the impressive sight of a brooding Leo Aleksandrov, pacing up and down like a tiger trapped in a too small cage.

As if sensing her presence, he stopped, and Lexi felt every one of her senses go on high alert as his eyes swept over her.

She normally had to buy a ticket to see a man like him as well. Usually on a movie screen. His virility was not at all adversely affected by the slightly crumpled shirt that clung to his wide shoulders. He'd rolled his shirtsleeves to reveal powerful, hair-roughened forearms; Lexi already knew the leashed power behind those arms and she shivered.

He broke her train of thought by shoving his hands into his pockets and she felt a flood of colour swamp her face as she realised that she'd been caught staring.

Pretending she wasn't at all flustered by his presence—

and wishing it was the truth—she smiled briefly and then turned away to search the room for her bag. 'Ty is asleep and I'm leaving.'

'You can't.'

She stopped in the middle of the room and looked at him. 'Excuse me?'

'I've dismissed Mrs Parsons.'

'Why would you do that? She was perfect.'

He regarded her levelly. 'She doesn't have a passport.'

Lexi didn't hide her shock. 'You dismissed a woman on the grounds that she's not well traveled? That's a bit narrow-minded isn't it?'

'I didn't dismiss her because of that,' he flashed at her, rubbing the back of his neck as if this whole conversation was terribly unnecessary. 'Look, perhaps you should sit down.'

'I don't want to sit down,' she flashed right back.

'I'm just as unhappy about this turn of events as you are but, realistically, it would have taken Ty too long to get used to her anyway.'

Lexi raised an eyebrow. He'd become an expert on his son now had he? 'So who are you going to get to help you out?' she asked, knowing before she'd even finished her question what his answer would be. 'No.' She shook her head and spoke before he'd even opened his mouth. 'That's not possible.'

'I will, of course, pay you for your time.'

'No!'

His lack of any response to her vehemence made her nervous. 'Anyway, I'm busy this weekend,' she said, hating that she felt as if she had to explain herself to this man. She moistened her lips and watched his eyes follow the movement. His gaze lingered and once again she wondered how his lips would feel against her own. Aimee's words about his sexual prowess popped into her head and her lips were once again bone-dry.

Oh, Lord, she had to get out of here.

His eyes returned to hers and she expelled a breath in a rush. 'Doing?'

'I'm going to Paris,' she declared. Deciding there and then that she'd give Simon a chance. It was time. Past time. And Simon was a saint compared to this man.

'Your friend seemed to think you hadn't yet made up your mind.'

Lexi frowned, wondering how he knew that. 'Aimee doesn't know everything,' she said, slightly flustered.

'And whom are you going to the city of light with, hmmm?'

Lexi felt her jaw clench at his supercilious tone. Simon would never have asked that question! He was well-mannered, polite, civilised, boring…

No. He was perfect.

Frustrated with her erratic thoughts, Lexi glanced towards the entrance foyer and wondered if she shouldn't just head for the door and be done with Leo Aleksandrov.

As if sensing her intention, his body tensed, his eyes fixed on her as if he would spring if she made the slightest movement to flee.

'You haven't answered my question.'

'Because it's none of your business!' she exclaimed hotly.

His penetrating gaze held hers but his body relaxed as if her answer had been predictable. Then he made her teeth clench even harder when he smiled knowingly. 'I'll send you and your lover first class next weekend.'

Lexi's eyebrows hit her hairline. 'You'll send?' she repeated indignantly. Just who did this man think he was?

'Pay. Organise.' He blew out a frustrated breath. 'Stop getting caught up on semantics.'

'Mr Aleksandrov, I—'

'I have to go to Greece for the weekend. I need somebody I can trust to take care of Ty.'

'You want me to go to Greece with you? For the long weekend?'

Lexi wasn't even prepared to go into the next room with him, let alone another country!

'No. I was taking Mrs Parsons to Greece because she is an unknown entity for both myself and Ty, and I felt it was better to have her close by. You, on the other hand, are not an unknown entity. You have looked after my son for two years and you will be perfectly fine to take care of him here, in London. And, as I said—' he paused, regarding her calmly '—I'll pay you. Well.'

'Is money your answer to everything?' Lexi snapped.

'Not *everything*, no.'

Her lips compressed at his sensually mocking smile.

'How much?' he asked with quiet confidence.

Lexi tried not to be intimidated by his size and understated force of will. Hadn't he realised that she wasn't the type of person who could be bought? Or was he the type of person who paid off everyone in order to get his own way? She wouldn't be at all surprised to find out that he was. 'You mean I can name my price?' she asked sweetly, as if she might actually be considering his offer.

'What's the number?' he demanded curtly, his smile flattening as if her answer had displeased him, though why that should be the case she hadn't a clue.

Lexi paused. Would he pay any figure? For a minute she was tempted to find out but she didn't play these types of games and it would give her more satisfaction to put him—and his open bank account—in their rightful place.

'The number is that there is no number. You don't deserve my help. Goodbye.'

Lexi didn't look at him as she picked up her bag and dropped her mobile phone inside. She was about to stride out of the door with her head held high when Leo's quiet voice stopped her.

'I might not. But Ty does.'

Lexi turned and stared at him incredulously. 'Are you try-ing to *emotionally* blackmail me now?'

'If it means you'll stay, yes.'

Lexi couldn't believe the gall of the man. Had he no shame?

'You get a girl pregnant and then don't even have the de-cency to get to know your own flesh and blood and now you'll do whatever it takes to have someone you don't even know take care of him. What kind of a man are you?'

He jammed his hands onto his hips and glared at her. 'Don't pass judgement on things you don't understand.'

'Oh, I understand all right,' Lexi fumed. 'I understand that your lifestyle is so precious you rejected an innocent child. Well, that's something you should have thought about *before* you got Amanda Weston pregnant, not *after*.'

'This has nothing to do with my lifestyle and everything to do with Ty's well-being.'

'And just how do you figure that?'

A muscle ticked in his jaw. 'I don't have to explain myself to you but I did not reject my son.'

'Oh? What would you call it?'

'Since he was born I have paid for every single thing he needs and I have six monthly reports carried out to ensure that he is safe and well cared for.'

'Reports that failed to inform you that his mother travels so often that his grandmother was his main carer until her death a fortnight ago.'

He had the grace to look uncomfortable, pulling at the col-lar on his shirt in a telling movement.

'And,' he continued, as if she hadn't spoken, 'I fully intend to have a relationship with him when he's older.'

Of all the...

'Older and less work?' she scoffed. 'He needs you now. A boy looks to his father as he grows up to figure out what it means to be a man. What kind of a man will he grow up to be with an absent father who never cared enough to spend time with him?' Lexi stopped, aware that her impassioned speech was about to get out of hand. But damn it, that was exactly what had happened to her brother, Joe, who had become lost and angry in his teenage years, even though Lexi and her mother had done their best to shield him from feeling rejected by his father.

'By all means say what you think, Miss Somers.'

Lexi shook her head. 'I don't believe in wasting time on empty words.'

'Rare for your sex, I have to say.'

'Oh—' Lexi shook her head '—I'll add chauvinist to your list of personal attributes, shall I?'

'I meant it as a compliment.'

'That's even worse!'

He leaned his hip against the edge of the sofa and cocked his head. 'Will I like any of the other things on your list?'

Lexi shot him a fulminating glare, feeling a little spent after her tirade. 'What do you think?'

He laughed and Lexi felt a tug of awareness low in her pelvis as he studied her, his casual stance and insolent regard making her aware of her femininity—her womanliness—in a way she hated. Making her think of sex—of all things!

She swallowed heavily and his eyes dropped to her throat and Lexi nearly raised her hand to cover it. What was he thinking about? Heat crept up her neck and she was afraid she might know.

'I think you're a woman with exacting standards that not many men manage to live up to.'

Lexi blinked. 'I think you'd fail to live up to most people's standards,' she retorted, stung a little by his assessment of her.

'You'd be surprised.'

'I'm not talking about the hundreds of women you go through like disposable razors.'

He smiled at that. 'Neither was I. And for your information, I use an electric.'

'Well, you didn't use it today,' she said hotly and then wished she hadn't when a sexy smile crossed his face. Damn. Now he probably thought she liked his stubble. Wanted to touch it, even. Huh! As if.

She tightened her hold on her bag, aware that the conversation was taking a dangerous turn. 'This is irrelevant.'

'I agree.' He pushed off from the sofa and sat down on it, his arms spread wide along the back like a sultan surveying his kingdom. 'So tell me, what is it going to take to get you to agree to take care of Ty this weekend?'

'Surely you have someone else who can help you out. A girlfriend, perhaps?'

'Is that your way of asking if I'm available, Miss Somers?'

Lexi glared at him. 'That's my way of asking if you have someone else to help you out. I would ask if you had a mother but I'm not sure you weren't hatched from an egg.'

Leo laughed, a deep, husky sound that sent tingles tracking down her spine. 'I'm single. But, even if I wasn't, bringing a girlfriend in at this late stage isn't really the answer, is it?'

It wasn't really a question and, worst of all, she knew he was right. Lexi glanced outside at the endless view of the night sky and felt oddly cornered. 'I can't just drop everything in my life to help you.'

'Think of it as helping Ty. You might find that more palatable,' he drawled.

Lexi made a derisive sound in the back of her throat and thought that if she wasn't such a nice person—and the thought of touching him didn't scare her so much—she'd smack him. 'Oh, you're good.'

'Thank you.'

'It wasn't a compliment.'

'I know.'

Just as he knew she was about to capitulate.

Lexi ground her teeth together and turned back and focused on the elegant dome of St Paul's Cathedral in the distance. Anything was better than looking at Leo sprawled on the sofa with arrogant nonchalance. No doubt he would be attending parties in Greece and having a lovely time. A lovely time without his son. Lexi drummed her fingers against her arm. Just like her father.

'What are you waiting for, Miss Somers?' Leo drawled, his accent giving the words a sexy edge. 'The stars to align?'

Lexi fumed. Arrogant so-and-so... And then an idea sprouted. What if he took Ty to Greece and had a chance to get to know his son? Would that change his attitude towards Ty? She didn't know, but it was worth a try and it was better than staying in London where there was no chance at all of that happening. Lexi didn't trust that Amanda could look after Ty without her mother around and, although Leo Aleksandrov didn't appear to be much better, she had to find out.

She turned back to consider him and tried to ignore sensations she would rather not feel shimmy down her spine as he looked back at her with lazy insolence. 'I'll do it if you take Ty with you.'

His eyelids lowered and when he raised them his eyes were no longer lazy or insolent, but hard and flat. 'Never been to Greece, angel?'

'Your list just got longer.'

Knowing the type of man he was she hadn't expected to win this point without a fight but, instead of arguing with her, he slowly rose to his feet, his eyes on her the whole time. Then he smiled, a killer's smile, and Lexi felt the cold plate-glass window through her clothing and realised she'd backed up a step. 'Careful, angel, you might fall.'

Lexi stiffened her spine and gave him a look that had been known to stay the rowdiest of children. 'I'm not afraid of you Mr Aleksandrov.' Or the way he called her *angel*, with the tiniest hint of sexual promise behind it.

Much, anyway.

She lifted her chin just a fraction as he continued to stare at her and then finally—thankfully—he nodded his head and gestured towards the door.

'Let me show you to your room.'

Lexi nearly threw her hands up in the air as she realised that she'd just inadvertently agreed to go to Greece with him. The *last* thing she wanted to do. But how could she say no, now? 'I must be mad,' she muttered under her breath, trailing him up the long corridor towards the bedrooms.

He stopped in front of the room next to the one Ty occupied.

Lexi folded her arms across her chest. 'Why do I have to stay here tonight if you're not leaving until the morning?'

'Insurance.'

'If I give my word then I keep it.'

'But you haven't given me your word.'

She very nearly stamped her foot at that. 'Are you always this argumentative?'

He leant against the door frame regarding her lazily. 'Funny, I was going to ask the same thing about you.' His voice held a husky quality she knew he'd probably used on a hundred other women and she hardened her resolve not to be affected by him.

Lexi took a deep breath. 'I give you my word I will return first thing in the morning.'

He shrugged. 'It doesn't matter. I need you here tonight in case Ty wakes up.'

Lexi wanted to argue with him but again he had a point. 'I don't have anything to wear to bed,' she mumbled, feeling utterly defeated and uncharacteristically irritable.

He held out his hand. 'Give me your address and keys and I'll send my driver to pick up whatever you need.'

'Why can't I go myself?'

'Because Ty might wake up.'

'I'll be an hour,' she said, completely exasperated.

'No.'

'Well, I'm not having someone I don't know go through my things.'

And she knew Aimee would be at Todd's by now so she couldn't very well call and get her to send her things over in a cab.

He looked down at her, his blue eyes twin pools of open sensuality. 'There's always your birthday suit.'

Lexi chose to ignore the dangerous gleam in his gaze and instead focused on the fact that this man was the worst type of playboy around. Then she remembered his suggestive comment in her office earlier. The man would probably have sex with a lamp post if it offered.

'I don't suppose one of your many girlfriends left a nightie I could borrow, did they?' she asked sweetly.

She was hoping he'd be a little embarrassed by her sarcasm, but instead the smile that curled the corners of his mouth was lethally sexy. 'I don't have *girlfriends*. But if you're referring to my many bed partners, I'll check.'

Lexi blew out a tank-load of air after he walked out and placed her bag on the embroidered silk bedspread and stood with her hands on her hips, wondering what she had got herself into. Then the hairs on the back of her neck rose and she didn't need to glance in the full-length mirror opposite to know he was back. She turned just in time to catch a wad of grey fabric he tossed at her. Holding it up, she saw it was a well-worn T-shirt someone might wear to the gym. 'This is yours,' she said huskily.

He looked at her through heavy-lidded eyes. 'And I'll dream about you in it all night, angel.'

'I don't find comments like that funny,' she reprimanded.

He smiled again and grabbed the door handle. 'Goodnight, Miss Somers. Oh—' he paused and Lexi felt her nerves, already jangling on a knife edge split down the middle '—in case I forget to tell you. I appreciate you staying. And tell lover boy I'm sorry for ruining his *plans*.' That last was spoken with not even a shred of sincerity. The louse.

She had fallen in with the devil and he was every bit as ruthless as myth suggested.

CHAPTER FOUR

LEXI didn't know what had woken her. The room was pitch-black so it wasn't yet morning and then she heard it again. A low, deep moaning sound.

'Ty.'

She stumbled out of bed and down the hall into his room, only to pull up short when she found him sound asleep, his face relaxed and peaceful in the soft glow of the bedside lamp.

Wondering if she had been so on edge with the whole 'sleeping at a billionaire's apartment' thing she had dreamt it, she was about to go back to bed when she heard it again.

'Leo.' She exhaled the word into the still night.

It was Leo, not Ty.

Lexi was momentarily paralysed in the middle of the darkened hallway, her heart thumping in her chest, indecision turning her into a statue. Then she heard him moan something that sounded like 'No, Sasha' and her legs carried her forward. She had always been a sucker for anyone in need. Stopping by roadsides to tend to hurt animals, collecting birds and trying to nurse them back to health. Once she had even demanded her mother stop the car and had rescued a lamb from a tangle of barbed wire. That lamb had been the love of her eight-year-old life, following her around in the garden every day as if it had imprinted on her.

Lexi forgot all about the lamb as she cautiously pushed

open the door to Leo's room and peered into the gloom. As her eyes adjusted, she could make out the richly furnished room, the curtains slightly parted, letting in a finger of light that fell across the end of an enormous bed.

The man in it moved restlessly and Lexi's eyes were drawn to the dark sheet that was tangled around his lower body. He lay on his back, one arm flung over his head, the other outstretched as if he was reaching for something. His chest was bare and utterly magnificent. Broad and lean with densely packed muscles beneath a light covering of chest hair that arrowed all the way down over his shadowed abdomen and beyond. And yes, it looked like he had a six-pack, she thought resentfully.

Lexi couldn't tear her eyes away as he shifted restlessly and remembered his question about whether she wanted to know what he slept in, hoping it was more than it looked like right now. He moaned again and rolled onto his side, fingers flexing and such a look of anguished despair on his face that Lexi's heart leapt and she automatically went to him. Whatever he was dreaming about, she felt sure he'd be better off awake than asleep.

Without even thinking, she reached down and placed her hand gently against the rounded ball of his shoulder.

Leo's reaction was instantaneous and, before she could draw breath, Lexi felt all the air whoosh out of her lungs as she found herself flat on her back beneath him. The expression on his face was so intense real fear rippled through her body.

'Mr Aleksandrov...Leo!' Lexi raised her hands to his naked chest and shoved against solid muscle that didn't give an inch. Heat spiked through her as her fingers slipped to the firm muscles of his shoulders, her lower body instantly clenching in reaction to the pressure of his hard, hair-roughened thighs pressed so intimately against her own. She tried to shift against him but she was literally pinned down and then she gasped, going stock-still as she felt the hardness of his erection pressed intimately between her thighs.

Oh, boy! Sensation the like she had never experienced arced through her body, turning it liquid, and she found herself involuntarily arching into him to assuage the ache that had sprung up deep in her pelvis.

She knew he felt her undeniably sexual response because the hand that gripped her arm moved to the nape of her neck and then fisted in her hair as he tilted her face up towards his. She wanted to tell him he was dreaming, but she lost all sense of reason as their eyes met in the dimly lit room and everything else faded. A breath shuddered through her and as his masculine scent acted like a drug on her senses she raised her face to receive the hard promise of his beautiful mouth.

It was as if all the tension of worrying about Ty and the second childcare centre, and Leo himself, coalesced into this moment and she gave herself over to the feel of him, moaning in pleasure as his lips crushed hers in a hard, possessive kiss.

Excitement barrelled through her and her hands slid up the smooth skin of his back, kneading and testing the muscles as she went. His skilful tongue demanded entrance to her mouth and when she gave it their muted groans mingled hotly in the otherwise silent room. Lexi felt as if she were on fire and when his hands started roaming over her body, learning her shape, it was all she could do not to tell him to hurry up as his hands moved closer and closer to her aching breasts. She shifted again, trying to make it easier for him, and then cried out as he sensed what she needed and shoved his hand up under her T-shirt and palmed her naked breast, the rough pad of his thumb drawing an animalistic sound from her throat as it swept across her painfully sensitive nipple.

'Oh!' Her legs scissored helplessly as she tried to lift her hips under the heavy weight of his, energy building inside of her and driving her towards a nirvana she'd never felt in a man's arms before.

'Easy,' his rough, sleep-laden voice whispered against her ear at the same time as one of his hands slid to her hips to stay her restless squirming.

But it was as if that one word had intruded on a magical, secret world and shattered it, reality returning with a sickening thud as she recalled where she was and who she was with.

Lexi pushed against his chest, her movements now frenzied for a different reason. 'Leo…Mr Aleksandrov. Get off. You've had a bad dream.'

He stilled instantly, hovering over her. Then his hand slipped from her bottom and he rolled onto his back.

Lexi jumped to her feet, her body feeling both hot and cold, her breathing ragged.

She didn't know what to say and wondered if he'd fallen back asleep and then she heard a young child's cry.

Ty.

Her thoughts a complete jumble Lexi did the only thing she could—she fled. Down the hall and straight into Ty's room.

Leo woke, feeling as if he had a hangover. He'd slept, fitfully and the recurring dream he'd had on and off since his brother's death had returned last night to haunt him. Of course he knew why, but he didn't want to think about that any more than he wanted to recall Sasha's death. A death he had inadvertently caused.

Leo turned his head to the side, as if that might dislodge the heavy guilt shrouding his heart, and caught the faintest trace of vanilla. Instantly another memory, a much more pleasurable one, slammed through his body and turned him as hard as stone.

Lexi Somers. She'd woken him and he'd momentarily thought it was his father attacking him. Had he hurt her? His mind sifted through the way he'd gripped her arms and brought her under him, the feel of her soft curves, the warm

V of her thighs as she'd cradled him intimately. Her taste... like the sweetest dessert...

Leo closed his eyes. There was something about her that had called to him since they'd met, so coming fully awake to find her under him had been too great a temptation to resist.

Chort vozmi.

He hadn't meant to kiss her but she'd said his name and lifted herself against him and what was a man supposed to do with that? The natural thing, of course.

Shafts of pleasure pulsed his groin as he recalled the feel of her mouth, the touch of her fingers.

He cursed again.

He couldn't remember ever being so turned on and if she hadn't stopped him he'd have buried himself inside her with no questions asked.

He pushed out of bed and padded into the bathroom. He didn't bother shaving and just rolled straight into the shower, welcoming the stinging bite of icy-cold water as it lashed his shoulders and overheated torso.

He leant his forehead against the wall and refocused his mind. He had a massive weekend planned. The maiden voyage of his new super-yacht, *Proteus*, which he had helped design and which he planned to use as a prototype to launch a new area of his business—building first-class environmentally powered yachts, ferries and ships. But first he had to convince the Greek environmental minister to sell him land in Thessaly for a new cutting-edge ethanol plant that could revolutionise the world's use of friendly fuel sources and one he needed to power his future ships.

Then there was Ty. For most of the night he'd tried to figure out how to handle things this weekend, Lexi's questions about why he didn't know him and her assertion of how much Ty needed him weighing heavily on his conscience. The trouble was he couldn't look at Ty without thinking of Sasha and he couldn't think of Sasha without getting emotional—

something that made his blood curdle. Emotions led to two things in his experience—weakness or violence—neither of which he wanted to let into his life. Which was why, despite his guilt, he'd stayed away from Ty. It would have been self-ish to have done anything else and the last time he'd acted selfishly his brother had lost his life.

Sighing heavily, he quickly pulled on his usual work at-tire and paused outside Ty's partially opened doorway. Not hearing any sound, he pushed the door further open to check if he was up.

What greeted him was the sweet curve of Lexi Somers' backside in the pale pink panties he'd shoved his hand into not a few hours ago. She was asleep on her side, his T-shirt bunched around her waist, her magnificent hair like a dark flag streaming out behind her, her body curved like a protec-tive bow around the small form of his son.

Leo felt a vice grip his heart and absently rubbed his chest. They both looked so innocent, so untouchable, and his mouth tightened as he forced himself to turn away and leave the room.

He should never have agreed to take them to Greece.

CHAPTER FIVE

A THOUGHT that had only grown stronger since his private plane had taken off from Heathrow an hour ago. Having worked with Danny for the past hour, he now cupped his hands behind his head and stretched his legs out in front of him.

His eyes cruised Lexi Somers' creamy complexion and lowered to her even white teeth as she smiled at something Ty said. They were sitting on the floor playing with toy cars Lexi had insisted he buy at the airport. She was wearing a plain T-shirt and denim jeans with her hair in a ponytail and should have looked like any other girl, but she didn't. She had an understated sexiness that she didn't seem to be aware of and while he appreciated that the scrubbed, girl-next door image turned some men on, he hadn't numbered among them before now.

He wondered how lover boy had taken the news that Paris was off and whether she had told him about the kisses they had shared the night before.

Probably not. Women were rarely honest about such things. And if she had, and lover boy was worth his salt, he would have come and laid Leo out cold. That was what he would have done if the situation had been reversed. If she was his and some guy had held her underneath him. But why was he thinking like this? She wasn't his. No woman was, or ever would be.

Leo scowled, annoyed with his thoughts and the way she had treated him with polite detachment since she had woken this morning. She hadn't mentioned what had transpired in his bed last night and he knew that was for the best. Why re-hash something he didn't care to explain, or repeat?

But he couldn't deny that her indifference rankled. They had stopped briefly at her apartment and, much to her cha-grin, he had accompanied her inside. He'd wanted to appease some latent curiosity about who she really was and what her motivation was for wanting to accompany him to Greece. Initially he had wondered if a latent gold-digger hadn't been hiding beneath her down-to-earth demeanour but, if any-thing her home only confirmed that she was most likely a nice girl. Soft furnishings, family photos on the mantelpiece in the sitting room, personal knick-knacks carefully placed on well-worn surfaces. The opposite of the various homes he kept around the world, which were always pristine and well ordered. Like his life usually was.

And hell, she hadn't even known who he was when they'd first met!

He glanced at Ty and cursed Danny's lack of foresight in sending him a nanny without a passport, knowing as he did that it wasn't Danny's fault. None of it was. It was his. And only he could fix things. The key now was to keep Lexi and Ty as far away from him as possible, which shouldn't be too hard. Yes, they'd be trapped together on his yacht for three days but the thing was as big as two football fields and con-sisted of eight levels. How hard could it be?

Bracing himself, Leo looked at his son. A boy he didn't want and a boy who hadn't asked to be born. Some might call it fate that Amanda had conceived on that one time they had had sex. He knew Lexi Somers thought Ty was suffer-ing from his absence but Leo didn't want to believe that. He had always believed he was doing the right thing, the hon-ourable thing, in staying out of Ty's life. In leaving him with his mother. But it seemed he might have been wrong and he couldn't stomach that. Couldn't stomach the thought of making a mistake again, of being responsible for another person's future happiness.

But still Lexi's words nagged at him. Was she right in suggesting that Ty's emotional needs were suffering? She was the expert who had cared for him for two years. Why would she say it if it wasn't true? And why had Amanda's mother been looking after Ty? He needed to find out more information, that was clear.

'Do you want to come join us?' The soft query from the angel—on the floor—brought his attention back to the present. His eyes met hers and he saw a wealth of questions in her guarded expression. She was trying to figure him out and that wasn't going to happen.

He stood up and pierced her with a warning look that had been known to make grown men quake.

The plane dipped slightly and one of the small cars Ty was playing with rolled towards him. Leo automatically bent to pick it up and then his eyes met his son's. They *were* blue, like his. And he could see now how Lexi had made the connection between them so quickly. On top of the eye colour, his son had the slashing eyebrows and strong bone structure that indicated his Cossack ancestry. Leo held his breath as dark images of Sasha at that age rolled into his brain like thunderclouds.

Ty moved towards him, intent on getting his car, and Leo felt the urge to get as far away from him as possible. Then he felt the unmistakable shift of the aircraft as it hit an air pocket, the bottom seeming to fall out of the plane. As if in slow motion, Ty stumbled, his little arms instinctively thrown forward to break his fall, and Leo reacted purely on instinct—reaching down and lifting his son into his arms before bracing himself against the side of the plane. They staggered together and Ty flung his arms around Leo's neck and for the first time ever

Leo breathed in his clean, little boy scent. His eyes closed, his body tensed. Within seconds the turbulence had passed, the plane once again steady.

'Are you okay?' Lexi's worried voice broke his paralysis and he opened his eyes to find her standing in front of him. He released a breath and clenched his jaw. No, he was not okay.

'Here.' He thrust Ty at her. 'Make sure he's strapped in at all times while the plane is in the air,' he grated coldly.

'Mr Aleksandrov...' He didn't know what she had been about to say and he didn't wait around to hear, making his way to his private bedroom for the rest of the journey. He slumped down on the edge of the bed and held his unsteady hands in front of him. Ty had felt so small and fragile. He spread his fingers and turned them back and forth, no longer seeing his own hands but those of his father's. How had he hit them at such a young age?

Athens was a revelation to Lexi. Hot, dry, crumbly...ancient! She loved it. Loved the busyness of the streets and the organised chaos of locals, tourists and Vespas winging in and out of the traffic.

She pointed things out to Ty as their taxi fought its way through the gridlock to God only knew where. She hadn't seen Leo after the incident on the plane and again found herself wondering at the type of man he was. She hadn't missed the pain behind his eyes as he had looked at Ty on the plane. Almost as if he was looking at someone else. A ghost. And did that have anything to do with his nightmare last night?

She knew from reading his biography online that he was an only child to 'warm and loving parents' who had died in a tragic accident when he was twenty. From there he had bought a scaffolding company and turned it into a global entity before expanding into hotels and construction. According to Wikipedia he had become the richest man in Russia by his thirtieth birthday, a position he still held five years on.

But if he came from such a loving family, why had he never accepted Ty as his son? What had gone wrong between him and Amanda? She hadn't been able to find any information about his connection to either one of them online, which was strange for such a high-profile person—which she now realised he was.

Not to mention the most exciting male she had ever set eyes on. Not that she planned to do anything about that. She only wished she wasn't so physically aware of him.

Like now, with her thigh touching the length of his in the taxi they had been forced to take from the airport. They were supposed to have ridden in Leo's helicopter, but as soon as Ty had heard the whine of the rotors he'd started to cry and Lexi had been pleasantly surprised when Leo had ordered a taxi instead. Now she was unpleasantly hot pressed against him in the confines of the small car and, from what she could tell by the amount of tapping Leo was doing on his phone, he hadn't noticed at all.

Finally, they alighted from the taxi and Lexi stretched and looked around. The port of Piraeus was teeming with activity and various large ferries and boats were docked at the tiny, industrious harbour, Athens rising behind her in a tier of mostly grubby, worn, age-old buildings.

'Look, Ty—' she pointed up the hill, where a cluster of deep green trees circled below the rocky ledge that housed the Parthenon and other ancient ruins '—the Acropolis.'

The little boy looked, but of course showed none of the excitement that she felt.

'Hurry up, it's hot,' Leo demanded grumpily behind her.

She turned and spotted the four casually dressed bodyguards she was still not used to flanking them.

'Of course it's hot.' She smiled, determined not to let his dark mood, or her own awareness of him as a man, colour her enjoyment of her surroundings. He had forced her to come, but it was her natural inclination to try and find the best in every situation. 'It's summer in Greece. Have you been to the Acropolis before?'

Leo scowled down at her. 'No.'

'Is this your first time in Athens, then?' she asked interestedly, shading her eyes against the sun as she looked up at him.

'I come here to work, not play.' He glanced at Ty and then back. 'Is he heavy?'

'No.'

'Good. Danny will give you a tour of *Proteus* and see to anything that you need.'

'Oh, what will you be doing?'

Her question caught Leo off guard and he didn't know if it was the heat of the sun, or her annoying serenity, or the fact he'd just spent the better part of an hour pressed up against her in a stifling taxi, but his patience was paper-thin. 'If I wanted to answer to someone, Miss Somers, I'd have a wife.'

Her eyebrows shot up and her exotic eyes, which had sparkled before as she'd enjoyed her surroundings, turned frigid. 'A novel concept for you, to be sure,' she retorted, stalking off ahead of him as if she were a queen dismissing a minion.

No, angel, you're the novel concept.

Simmering with frustration, Leo found himself absently watching the provocative sway of her hips in jeans that were surely a size too small before indicating to two of his security detail to follow her.

He boarded his yacht and his captain and two engineers were waiting to give him a personal tour. When that was done, he headed to his private office to work.

Only his mind wouldn't focus and by nightfall he had given up. Tomorrow he would have up to thirty guests enjoying a weekend on-board and he would need to be in top form for the meetings he had planned.

Even though it was late, he decided to stop by the pool deck for a drink. It was empty, the bar closed and most of the sun loungers packed away for the night. He took a seat in a deck-chair under the awning, out of sight of the prying lens of any roving paparazzi that had got wind he was on-board, and enjoyed the peaceful sound of the sea slapping against the sides of the nearby vessels and the distant rumble of city traffic.

He heard a door behind him slide open and presumed it was a steward come to see if he wanted something to drink. Then he heard the soft sound of flip-flops crossing the deck and knew it wasn't a staff member. He watched Lexi Somers stroll to the railing and gaze out over the harbour and back towards Athens.

There wasn't anything overtly sexual about her in hot pink leggings and a jade-green oversized shirt but he couldn't take his eyes off her. She had been getting under his skin since the moment he had met her. But he couldn't for the life of him understand the attraction. She didn't appear to be like any other woman he'd met before. She was beautiful but didn't flaunt it, she seemed intelligent and switched on and yet she played children's games with ease and enthusiasm. And she spoke her mind—a quality he had never admired in a woman before.

In some ways she reminded him of the way his mother had been with Sasha—gentle and loving. Although Leo knew that his mother must have cared for him too, he knew that she had never approved of him. Where Sasha had been gentle, he had been rough. Where Sasha had been passive, he had been aggressive. He remembered that too often she had told him he was just like his father and she hadn't meant it as a compliment.

He returned his attention to Lexi Somers, who looked almost lost as she gazed out over the water, and he wondered if she was thinking about Paris. About her Parisian lover. Missing him, even.

'Unless your intention is to be on the cover of the morning paper tomorrow, I suggest you stand back from the railing.'

'Oh.' She jumped at the sound of his voice and squinted

to where he sat in the semi-darkness, the deck lit only by a few well-spaced down-lights.

'I didn't see you sitting back there in the dark.'

Leo crossed one foot over his opposite knee, his hands clasped behind his head as he slouched a little further into his deckchair. 'So it seems.'

'I was trying to see if I could see the Parthenon at night. I hear it's beautiful.'

'All you'll see is camera flashes going off if you're not careful. Or is that what you want?'

'Oh, yes, that would be great,' she scoffed. 'As you can see, I've dressed for the occasion.'

Leo reluctantly ran his eyes over her. She looked more than fine to him. 'They won't know who you are anyway. And since I wasn't standing beside you they're unlikely to dig. Most likely they'll assume you're staff. Except if you wander around in that red bikini you had on today. I don't usually let my staff dress like that when they're working.'

'Lucky I'm not staff.'

'Your choice,' he said, reminding her of her wish not to be paid for the weekend. Which still irked him. If he was paying her the lines of their relationship would be clearer and he wouldn't always be thinking of crossing them.

She narrowed her eyes as she walked towards him. 'I didn't see you by the pool earlier today.'

'I was on the bridge.'

'Spying?'

'Going over the itinerary with my captain,' he advised curtly.

'I was teasing,' she informed him and Leo felt his teeth gnash together at her amused expression.

She wandered over and stood beside his table. 'Ty loves the water. In summer we get out buckets and let the kids play with water in the sandpit and he's first in line. He also loves to run. I don't know if you noticed but when he gets going he's—'

'What's that you're holding?'

She glanced at the white plastic object in her hand. 'A monitor.'

Leo frowned, immediately suspicious. 'For what?'

'Ty. It was one of the things I requested on the list I put together this morning.'

'What's it for?'

'If he wakes up and cries out I'll hear him. It's a bit like a walkie-talkie but it only transmits signals one way.'

'You can't be available to him day and night,' he said somewhat churlishly.

'Somebody has to be.'

Leo ignored the shaft of guilt that speared his gut and made a mental note to ask his housekeeper to organise someone to assist her during Ty's sleep time.

Just then a steward came out and asked if they would like drinks and Lexi surprised him by ordering a chamomile tea.

'It's very calming. You should try some.'

'Are you suggesting I'm not calm?'

She tilted her head and her long hair spilled over one shoulder. 'I don't think I'll answer that lest we start an argument.'

'You're here. That's almost guaranteed to start one.'

She smiled. 'Now *you're* teasing.' Her eyes sparkled as she tried not to laugh at him again.

He wasn't, but he decided to let it ride. Sitting out on his deck on a moonlit night with a beautiful woman he did not want to be attracted to was not conducive to bringing out his sense of humour.

'I tried to find you earlier tonight.'

'Why?'

She gripped the back of the deckchair in front of her. 'I wanted to ask you if you would like to read Ty a bedtime story.'

'I was in a meeting,' he said, his voice sharper than he intended.

She tilted her head as she considered his answer. 'Would you have done it if you hadn't been in a meeting?'

He was shocked when she called his bluff.

'No.'

He could see that his curt reply had surprised her and he was glad. Don't ask questions, *moya milaya,* that you don't want answers to.

'Why not?' she asked softly.

Did the woman never give up? Did she somehow expect him to open up and spill his guts all because she had asked an insightful question in a nice voice?

Leo leaned forward, his elbows on his knees, annoyed with himself and her. 'You really want to know?'

She stepped forward, drawn in. 'If you want to tell me.'

'Take a seat.' He indicated the deckchair next to his, his voice low.

She looked from him to the chair and back, a shade warily, and Leo felt some primitive thrill of a bygone age rise up inside himself. The lure was set and she just had to take two more steps and then he'd trap her and tell her to mind her own business. That he would not discuss his relationship with his son with her or anyone else. He might even kiss her as well. Just to find out if she really did taste as good as his recall said she did.

She hesitated beside the chair, but he could tell she hadn't taken the bait. More was the pity. 'There's always tomorrow night.'

He raised a mocking eyebrow. 'To take a seat?'

Her eyes flashed. 'To read him a story.'

'Alas, I'm all out of fairy tales, angel.'

She pursed her lips at the pet name he'd given her and he cocked his head as he considered her. 'Is that why you became a childcare worker? You like fairy tales.'

'I like children. They're honest and pure.'

Like her? He leant back in his chair. 'Could it be that you prefer dealing with children more than adults?'

'Of course not.'

'Of course yes!' He gave an unrepentant grin at her fervent denial, enjoying himself all of a sudden.

Something her next sharp words ground into dust.

'Do you have any intention of spending time with your son this weekend?'

'I didn't think you wanted an argument,' he sneered.

'I don't. I just think it's important.'

'You're not here to orchestrate a family reunion, Miss Somers, so stop trying.'

Her eyes glittered angrily in the low light. 'You would have to be a family in the first place for me to be able to do that,' she blazed back at him.

Fortunately the steward arrived with their beverages and eased the tension that had hardened the air between them. He could feel Lexi watching him but he ignored her and picked up his bottle of mineral water, lamenting the fact that he had given up alcohol seventeen years ago and wishing it was a full bottle of Stolichnaya instead.

'I don't understand you,' she said, breaking the silence once the steward was safely out of earshot. 'You grew up in what sounds like a wonderful family and yet you treat Ty as if he doesn't exist.'

Leo observed her with a level of calmness he was far from feeling. 'I won't discuss my relationship with my son with you, Miss Somers,' he said through clenched teeth, 'so stop prying.' She pulled the chair out opposite him and Leo felt as if a rock had settled in his stomach. She had an uncanny knack of making him feel guilty about Ty but she didn't know the truth behind his decision. She didn't know what he was capable of and for a split second he considered telling her. Which was madness! He never talked about himself. Ever.

And he sure as hell wouldn't be telling Lexi Somers about it either.

He was just about to return to his suite when she bent one knee up and rested her chin on it. 'Do you ever do anything besides work?'

A myriad of answers formed in his head but they would be dangerous to play to. Because while intellectually he had already decided to ignore the chemistry between them, physically he had already started to respond to the hint of vanilla carried across to him on the warm evening air.

'Sometimes,' he said evenly.

'Like what?'

Like sex. His nostrils flared as the thought hardened his groin. *Right here and right now if she were willing.* He saw her eyes widen slightly and knew she had picked up on the direction of his thoughts. Maybe the fact that he was staring at her mouth wasn't very subtle.

'Looking for a demonstration, angel?'

The air between them became charged and he noticed her running her silver necklace between her fingers.

Oh, boy.

In trying to find out more about him and how best to influence him into spending time with Ty, Lexi had inadvertently jumped into a minefield with a man who knew where all the loaded mines were.

He wasn't trying to hide his sexual interest in her and she was shocked to see it. She had convinced herself that what had happened last night was because they had both been half asleep and that the chemistry she felt was entirely one-sided, but perhaps that wasn't the case. Or perhaps he was just bored and toying with her to avoid talking about himself. That would make more sense but, whatever it was, she was just glad he hadn't remembered his nightmare last night or what had followed.

It would also help if she could stop thinking about how well the man kissed and how hard his muscles had felt pressing her into the bed. God, he made her feel desperate for sex and already her body felt hotter, heavier. But she wasn't any good at sexual banter and her cup clattered as she put it down. 'I think I might go to bed,' she said, inwardly grimacing at her gaucheness.

'Scared, angel?'

'Of?' she asked carelessly, glancing everywhere but at him.

'The way I make you feel, for one.' His voice was a lazy purr.

'Excuse me?' She coughed out a laugh as if he'd just told her an implausible joke.

His smile said he didn't believe her for a second and his stunning eyes glittered in the low light, laughing at her.

'So tell me,' he said in a way that put her even more on edge, 'how did lover boy take your rejection last night?'

'It wasn't a rejection.' She bristled at his arrogant confidence. Well, it was, she supposed, but it had nothing to do with him. 'And his name is Simon.'

'That wasn't what I asked.'

'I'm not telling you,' she said, wishing now that she had headed for her room when the thought had first occurred to her.

'It's different when the boot's on the other foot, isn't it, angel?'

'Stop calling me angel,' Lexi fumed, feeling decidedly unsettled by his nettling. Especially when she conceded that *maybe* he had a point. If she wouldn't answer his questions, why should he answer hers? 'And of course he wasn't happy, but he understood.'

It was one of the qualities that had initially drawn her to Simon. Calm, methodical, rational, dependable.

'Understood what?' Leo's dark voice broke into her thoughts. 'That he came second to me?'

Oh, what an ego!

'That isn't what happened at all,' Lexi countered, uncomfortably aware that Simon would *always* come second to him if a woman had a choice.

'No?' He gave a wolfish smile.

'No.'

'So you told him what happened in my bed last night then?' he asked silkily.

Lexi's breath lodged in her throat. Damn it, he *had* remembered what had happened and had only been *toying* with her. How had she thought even for a second that a man like him would be interested in her as a woman?

'Your list just got longer,' she said smartly.

He disconcerted her by laughing. 'Admit it, angel, you're attracted to me.'

'You're wrong about that.' She cleared her throat and nearly spilt her cup of tea.. 'I would never be attracted to a man like you.' It was a lie, but oh, she wished it wasn't.

'Trying to insult me to deflect how you feel isn't very original,' he said softly.

'Neither is the size of your ego.'

Rather than be insulted, he laughed again. 'I liked you in my bed,' he said softly.

His lips curved into a lazy grin that made her stomach flip.

'I was *not* in your bed,' she insisted sharply, frustrated by her body's automatic reaction to his suggestive tone. She had yet to find anything positive about this man and yet her body responded to his every move as if he was master of it. How could that happen when she didn't even like him?

'No?' He scratched the sexy stubble on his jaw with well-shaped, capable fingers. 'Then my imagination is very vivid because I can still taste your sweet mouth under mine.'

Lexi stifled a gasp. 'You were having a nightmare.'

'Those kinds of dreams are never nightmares, angel.'

She forced herself to hold his sensual gaze and decided

the best thing she could do was to ignore his sexual banter. 'Do you have them often?' she asked, trying to redirect the conversation.

'Erotic dreams? Not since I was a youth.'

'Nightmares.'

His eyes turned flinty. 'You were mistaken if you thought I was having a nightmare. Perhaps you're just looking for an excuse as to why you kissed me last night.'

'*You* kissed *me*.'

'That's not how I remember it.' He gazed at her through sleepy eyes.

It wasn't exactly how she remembered it either.

'You were asleep. I was… We were both half asleep,' she babbled stupidly.

'And it was a lovely way to be woken up. I won't be at all upset if you do it again.'

'I would never go into your room voluntarily. You called out in your sleep. Someone named Sasha.'

'You must have been mistaken. But now *I'm* going to bed.' He stood up abruptly and towered over her. 'Care to give me a goodnight kiss, angel?'

Lexi stiffened at the audacious invitation and the instaneous 'yes' that leapt into her mind.

'Just in case you're labouring under the misapprehension that I find you funny, Mr Aleksandrov, I don't.'

She held her breath as his smouldering gaze lingered on her mouth. 'Now there's a pity. We might have had some fun together if you should ever lighten up.'

If she…? Lexi's face paled as his offhanded comment bit deep and shattered her confidence.

Arrogant, stupid ass!

CHAPTER SIX

THE next morning Lexi didn't see Leo at all, which was a good thing, she told herself.

She was still frustrated at their conversation last night, realising too late that he'd used sexual innuendo to avoid talking about Ty and then had inadvertently hit on the same complaint Brandon had had with her. And if at times she appeared uptight it was because she'd learned to guard her feelings from a young age, her father's betrayal having sapped all the happiness from her home for a long time after he'd left.

She frowned. Maybe she should just give up on her goal to reunite father and son. Maybe it would be better if she avoided Leo at all costs. Ty wasn't her child and she knew better than to become too attached to a child who was in her temporary care. And maybe Ty was better off with Amanda. It certainly seemed that way with the little interest Leo continued to display towards his son.

Yes, she'd stop playing some modern version of Mary Poppins and keep well away from Leo Aleksandrov. Right after she spoke to him this morning about the young Greek girl, Carolina, he had apparently assigned to assist her. As if she needed an assistant!

She rounded a corner of the yacht and smiled politely as yet another group of uber-trendy individuals passed her in the corridor.

Leo's weekend guests had arrived throughout the morning, some joining her and Ty by the pool and slipping into holiday mode as if they'd been born to it. One woman in particular, the supermodel Katya—no last name required, which was so yesterday, Lexi thought churlishly—had immediately rubbed her up the wrong way. Though whether that was because she had clung to Leo like the last autumn leaf on a tree or because she had that air of practised superiority about her Lexi wasn't sure.

Oh, who was she kidding? She'd been put out because of the way *Leo* had looked at *her*. A woman who was tall, stunning and exactly his type. Lexi wondered if she was his current mistress and felt her mouth pinch together. If she was, he was more of a cad than she had given him credit for. Flirting outrageously with her—kissing her and touching her—while his girlfriend was in transit from America.

Lexi wandered from deck to deck and had no idea what level she was now on. She was almost out of breath and finally understood that the central glass elevator, beautifully inlaid with designer plants and flowers, was not just a showpiece for guests to appreciate as they wandered past!

This ship, which Leo called a yacht, had so many rooms it was more like a floating castle. A very sleek and richly furnished castle with more natural stone and marble than a Renaissance church.

She stopped in the doorway of an elegant sitting room and noticed the supermodel, Katya, at the far end, shaking her finger at a young staff member, who looked as if she was about to collapse.

Used to sorting out all kinds of problems Lexi didn't think twice before approaching to offer her assistance. The younger girl, whom she had met downstairs earlier, looked at her with open relief.

'Hi there; what seems to be the problem?' she asked pleasantly.

The supermodel swung around sharply at the sound of her voice. She looked Lexi up and down as if she was considering whether or not she was worthy of an answer, and then waved her hand dismissively at the other girl.

'The *problem* is that laundry staff are not supposed to occupy the same room as a guest.'

'I was delivering t-t-towels to the second pool area,' the young girl stammered.

'Does this look like a swimming pool to you?' the model snapped.

'Again, I'm sorry ma'am. I got lost.'

Lexi threw the younger girl a sympathetic glance but Katya wasn't finished reprimanding her.

'You pass them onto the steward anyway, you imbecile. You shouldn't be above deck yourself.'

Not above deck in this glorious weather! Was that true? Lexi was flabbergasted and appalled at the model's attitude in equal measure. 'Excuse me, but that's no way to speak to anybody,' she reproved, not caring if this woman *was* Leo's latest mistress.

The model's eyes widened at her tone. 'And who are you to speak to me like that?' She regarded Lexi as if she were an ugly bug—which was exactly how she felt, standing beside the couture-clad model wearing a chain store white vest top and khaki shorts. 'Aren't you some sort of servant yourself? You shouldn't be up here either.'

Lexi ignored the comment and was about to offer to take the towels and leave the model to her own horrible company when Leo's deep voice cracked through the air like a whip.

'Katya.'

Lexi noticed the model curve her body into a provocative pose as Leo approached. He looked fit and utterly male in navy trousers and a crisp white dress shirt. 'If I ever catch you speaking to my staff like that again it will be your last time on one of my yachts.'

'Leo, darling,' the model cooed, 'I was just informing these girls of the rules and they got upset.'

'You were being a bitch. Leave us.'

'Leo!' She tried to hook her arm through his but he cast her a look that would have turned mortals into stone.

She sniffed and blinked a sexy glance from beneath her thickly coated lashes. 'I'll be by the pool.'

They all watched her saunter out of the room and Leo turned to the laundress. 'I apologise, Stella, for any offence my guest may have caused you. Here, let me take those.'

He knew the laundress's name? Lexi wouldn't have believed it if she hadn't heard it with her own ears. *And* he was going to carry towels?

'Thank you, Mr Aleksandrov.' Stella handed over her bundle and all but curtsied before scurrying out of the room.

'Nice company you keep,' Lexi said.

'Not everyone behaves like that.'

They stared at each other for a moment too long and then Lexi remembered that she'd been looking for him. 'I wanted to ask why you assigned Carolina to assist me.'

He hesitated before answering. 'You have a problem with my decision?'

How did he know she had a problem with it when she'd tried to keep her query light? 'No. Well, yes. I'm a qualified childcare provider. I can look after one child with my hands tied behind my back.'

'Ah, you think I'm questioning your professional integrity.'

'Aren't you?'

'No, Lexi. I've seen how good you are with Ty. But I don't expect you to be on call for him twenty-four seven. Carolina is to relieve you while he sleeps.' He looked down at the monitor in her hand and his brows drew together. 'Is that what he's doing now?'

'Yes. He usually has a midday nap at the centre and I thought the consistent rhythm would help him adjust.'

'Then shouldn't Carolina have this device?'

'Carolina is sitting in with him and I'll return once I hear him wake up.'

He nodded. 'Even better. Have you had lunch?'

Lexi paused, something in his expression when she had said Carolina was in with Ty sparking an instinctive knowledge deep inside her. 'You do care about him, don't you?'

Leo blinked slowly, his expression inscrutable. 'I repeat— have you had lunch?'

Lexi sighed, realising her comment had completely ruined the brief moment of accord between them.

'No, I haven't had lunch.'

'Come. It is being served on the pool deck today.'

Lexi shook her head. Having decided that she needed to keep her distance from him, the last thing she should do was sit down to lunch at his table. 'I can eat in the mess hall with the other staff.'

Leo was about to object when Danny walked into the room. 'Everyone is seated for lunch, Leo.'

Leo nodded but didn't take his eyes off Lexi. 'You will dine at my table.'

Again she shook her head. He was too virile, too male. And the way he towered over her made her too aware of her own femininity, her own *vulnerability* in his magnetic presence. 'You were the one who told me I was staff.'

'And you were the one who reminded me that you weren't,' he informed her silkily.

Lexi sighed. 'I'm hardly dressed for a proper luncheon.'

Leo slowly ran his sizzling gaze down over her casual clothing and down her bare legs and sandalled feet and all the way back up again.

'You look fine.' His voice was gruff, the tone sending frissons of sensation skittering into her belly. Given that she found it hard to keep her eyes off him she would really rather eat a hundred miles from where he was.

She was about to try some other excuse when her phone rang and she reached into her pocket and pulled it out. Recognising the number of her builder, Lexi smiled with relief. She'd been waiting for his call since yesterday and mentally crossed her fingers that he had good news about the renovations on the new centre. 'Excuse me,' she murmured, 'but I have to take this.'

Leo scowled as he watched Lexi Somers' toned legs take her to the other end of the room, wondering who was on the other end of the phone that had made her face light up with such obvious delight.

Her lover?

He felt his good mood at the progress he'd made in his meetings this morning evaporate into thin air.

His scowl deepened when he saw Lexi's expression turn worried. Was lover boy giving her a hard time? And why did it rankle so much to see her so affected by it?

'What's up?' Danny looked at him quizzically and Leo realised that Danny had picked up on his keen interest in the obstinate brunette.

'Nothing. Just see that Lexi Somers has lunch at my table,' he said curtly.

He stalked off but instead of his mood picking up when Lexi did eventually grace his table with her presence, it only worsened. She was too natural and friendly for his liking. A little *too* natural and *too* friendly with the American film-maker, Tom Shepherd. And he didn't like that he'd noticed and liked even less that it was bothering him so much. He couldn't concentrate on the lavish meal his world-class chef had prepared, or the conversation that was going on around him.

All he could hear were snippets of conversation as Tom charmed her with stories about the documentary film he was producing—the one Leo was bankrolling—and how interested she was in it, her smile generous and warm, her golden eyes sparkling as she sipped her Riesling and unself-consciously de-veined prawns before popping them into her mouth. He could see Tom was fascinated with her and it would appear that his interest was reciprocated. And where was her loyalty to her Parisian lover as she flirted with Tom Shepherd?

Leo snorted out a quiet breath. She was no different from any other female who saw a better meal ticket come along. But, if that was the case, why hadn't she latched onto him? Because he knew, without conceit, that he was the best meal ticket on this yacht, even with some of the world's most influential men currently dining at his lavishly set table.

Logically, Leo knew he was being ridiculous since he'd already decided not to pursue her, but for once logic and his libido were diametrically opposed to each other. He couldn't look away as Tom touched Lexi's arm and leant close to indicate for her to look at a flock of pelicans soaring overhead. The whole table seemed mesmerised by the majestic birds but all Leo could do was stare as Lexi's face lit up. Unbidden, an image of her pale figure in his bed the other night came to mind, her hair spread over his pillow just before he'd speared his fingers into it and crushed her mouth beneath his. The way she had met his demands with a hunger that had seemed to match his own. Her soft mews of pleasure as his hand had cupped her breast, the silky skin of her bottom—

'Did you say something?' Danny murmured.

'Only that I should have let her go to the mess hall,' Leo growled, turning away from the amused glint in his EA's eyes and striking up a conversation with the Greek minister about the reason they were even able to watch birds circling above his damned yacht this weekend.

'Jet skis?' Leo repeated blankly as he stared at Tom Shepherd.

'Yeah, you know? Motorbikes on water.' Tom smirked. 'You don't mind if we take them out for a spin, do you? Lexi's a jet ski virgin and I said I'd show her what she was missing.'

Leo's jaw clenched at Tom's provocative comment. The yacht was temporarily anchored between two small private islands and the water was deep enough so there wasn't any reason for him to say no. But he wanted to.

'I need to speak with Miss Somers.' He flashed his teeth in a tight smile. 'Take someone else.'

Before Tom could stage his protest, Danny stopped at his side. 'Leo, the men are waiting in the stateroom to resume the meeting, as you requested.'

Leo muttered a curse under his breath. If he'd been dealing with Australians or the English the negotiations would have been finished by now. No way would they have pulled up stumps to be wined and dined with a decadent lunch midway through an important meeting. No, they would have put up with soggy sandwiches and finger food at the conference table until the deal was signed, sealed and delivered. Then gone out and got drunk by way of celebrating.

'Well, that settles it.' Tom clasped Lexi's shoulder lightly and Leo was glad to see her eyes flicker to Tom's hand uncertainly as she shifted out from under his hold. 'Come on,' he said to Lexi. 'I promise you'll love it.'

'Where's Ty?' Leo found himself asking. 'Your charge.'

Lexi looked at him but he couldn't read her expression. 'He's still asleep. He probably will be for another forty minutes at least.'

With no other way to prevent her from going with Tom, Leo signalled a nearby steward. 'Have the jet skis organised for Mr Shepherd and any other interested guests.' Then he turned back to Tom. 'Be careful.'

Tom shook his head as if Leo was mad. 'I always am, man; don't sweat it.'

Leo shoved his hands into his pockets and watched as Tom cupped Lexi's elbow and led her towards the elevator, annoyed when she didn't shake him off the second time.

'I don't think he's realised she's off-limits yet,' Danny murmured.

Leo shot him a warning look. 'That's because she isn't.'

Leo stormed down to the conference room and ignored the irrational urge to go after Lexi and take her out on the thing himself.

Not that he wanted to go out on a damned jet ski. He wanted to focus on what he enjoyed most—business. He'd been working for two years on developing this ethanol plant and he wasn't about to jeopardise it to have fun in the sun.

What did he care about the sparkling blue waters of the Aegean, or the sandy islands surrounding him? To him, this location was just another venue to continue his business dealings. Relaxing was something he did after hours either at the gym or with a woman. Lazing around on a beach or riding a jet ski had never been on his list of things to do.

But half an hour later he was glad he'd insisted Danny stay in the meeting because he was the only one holding it all together. For some reason, Leo couldn't seem to get his brain into gear. Maybe he'd had too much sun upstairs because the state-of-the-art airconditioning wasn't doing anything to cool his blood. Nor was the buzzing of the jet skis and the delighted catcalls and squeals of his guests as they enjoyed themselves outside his window.

Leo paced around the airconditioned room and understood how a jungle cat felt locked up in a zoo.

He noticed the conversation had stopped and waved his hand absently. 'Carry on,' he said to the Greek minister's young and ambitious lawyer. 'I'm listening.'

He ignored Danny's concerned glances and stalked over to the window, watching as four jet skis were lined up ready to race.

One of the men yelled, 'Go' and they all gunned the engines, the skis lurching full speed over the water. Leo's eyes cut to Tom, who had Lexi on the back without a life jacket.

A cold sense of dread settled over his skin. He should have stopped her from going. Or, better yet, gone with her. His instincts had been on high alert and if she got hurt it would be his fault. He didn't question his need to protect her and nor did he ignore it. The last time he had, he'd lost his brother.

'Take five, gentlemen,' he threw over his shoulder as he marched out of the room.

CHAPTER SEVEN

HE MADE it to the lower deck just as Tom hit a rough patch of water and the ski lifted into the air and landed at a sharp angle. Leo's heart flew into his mouth as Lexi screamed and flew off the side of the machine and disappeared under the water. For a split second he was paralysed as the rider behind Tom rode dangerously close to the wake.

Then he moved. Jumped onto the lower ramp and grabbed the remaining jet ski from one of the attendants, flying out over the sparkling sea to where Lexi had gone under. The other riders hadn't realised what had happened and Tom had just got his machine under control when Leo reached the place Lexi had gone under.

Fortunately, her head broke the surface but Leo could see she had swallowed water and was having trouble breathing.

He cut the engine and leaned down over the side. 'Lexi, give me your hand,' he shouted. She looked disoriented and flailed around and Leo hooked his arm around her torso and hauled her up in front of him.

'Is she all right?' Tom called out as he pulled up alongside.

'You'd better hope so, Shepherd,' Leo snarled. He quickly ran his eyes over Lexi, but he couldn't get a good look at her as she curled over his arm retching violently.

Leo cursed, ordering Tom to go back and get the in-house doctor. He held Lexi against his chest as he yanked on the throttle and headed towards the nearby island. It was closer than the yacht and he wanted to get her horizontal as quickly as possible.

The small curved inlet was deserted and once he hit the shallow water he jumped down and swung Lexi up into his arms. He ran through the breakwater and dropped to his knees and gently laid her onto the sand. She was shaking with reaction, her clothes clinging to her like a second skin, but other than that she didn't appear injured.

'Did the ski hit you anywhere?' he asked hoarsely.

She shook her head and winced a little. 'No.' She raised a shaky hand to push her hair out of her eyes and he leaned forward and did it for her. 'I think I just got winded when I hit the water.'

She tried to sit up but Leo held her down with an unsteady hand on her shoulder. 'Lie back. Shepherd's getting the doctor.'

'I'm okay.' She moved her arms and legs carefully to make sure. Leo's heart was still lodged in his throat and adrenalin coursed through his blood.

'Just keep still,' he growled, the wealth of emotion in his voice raising her eyes to his. He couldn't look away and nor, it seemed, could she. The world receded; even the relentless heat from the sun in a cloudless blue sky faded into the background as Leo felt emotions he didn't want to name roll through him, searching for purchase.

Without conscious thought, he raised an unsteady hand to the side of her face. 'You could have been killed.' His voice was rough and heat arced between them as he gazed into golden eyes framed by long, wet, spiky lashes. His fingers stroked into her hair and she nestled her cheek into the curve of his palm.

Fascinated, Leo watched the gold of her eyes become eaten up by black, leaving only a ring of emerald-green, and his body caught fire at the implicit message her dilated pupils transmitted to him. Green. Her eyes turned green with passion.

As if somehow driven by the need to affirm that she was okay, Leo's eyes dropped to her parted lips seconds before his head followed.

He didn't know if she too was driven by the scare of her accident but her mouth flowered beneath his and her hands speared into his hair as she answered the urgent demand of his lips.

One of his arms banded around her lower back as he raised her to him and he felt the tips of her breasts nestle against his chest as she strained closer, the heat of her body burning through her flimsy vest top and his shirt as she caught fire in his arms.

Her urgency more than matched his and he revelled in the way she tried to take charge of the kiss, her thumbs gliding over his cheekbones as she held his face steady while she sipped and nipped at his mouth. He let her play for maybe a second before crushing her mouth beneath his. She moaned and he answered that sound of pleasure with a low groan of his own, pressing her back into the sand and taking control of the kiss.

This was total insanity but he couldn't deny how much his body ached to take her. His tongue curled around hers and his mouth turned hard as the same primitive hunger he'd felt with her the other night took hold and threatened to consume him, all sense of reason and caution flying into the air to be fried by the midafternoon sun.

He didn't know how it was possible for the sound of the approaching jet ski to be heard over the loud beating of his heart but fortunately it brought him to his senses and he wrenched his mouth from hers, his body throbbing with unslaked desire.

Her mouth was kiss-swollen and he knew the good doctor would know what had happened even if he hadn't seen them and Leo cursed his own stupidity. The woman had nearly died in an accident and he'd what—tried to ravish her?

Emotions exploded through him and landed with unerring accuracy on Tom Shepherd as he barrelled up the sand towards them. Rage the like he couldn't remember took over from lust and circuited his body. His muscles tensed and for a split second he contemplated meeting him halfway and putting his fist through his face.

Lexi must have sensed his intent because she placed her warm palm on his forearm. 'Don't.' That softly spoken plea brought him back to his senses and stopped him in his tracks. A bar room full of men hadn't been able to stop him after he'd located the man responsible for the death of his uncle in a work-related accident but this woman could contain him with the slightest touch. Of course he'd been irrational with pain at the time his uncle had died, but somehow the emotions he'd felt today when he'd watched Lexi go under hadn't been that much different. Which was absurd. He'd loved his uncle and didn't care a whit about Lexi Somers.

'Lexi, are you okay?' Tom's concern was palpable and Leo shook off his disconcerting thoughts and pierced him with a look. If he but knew it, Tom Shepherd was only standing because of the woman he'd nearly killed. He hadn't put a life jacket on Lexi and Leo knew why. And he knew why Tom had gone extra fast to make her cling to his back. Had she enjoyed it, pressed up against Tom's back as she'd held tight? Had she been thinking of *Tom* when she'd responded to *his* kisses moments ago? Leo inwardly cursed the direction of his thoughts. This sense of jealousy—because he recognised that was what it was even though he had never experienced it before—was so unlike him. Women were always easy to come by and easy to let go.

Unused to feeling so out of balance, Leo turned his anger on her. 'Why the hell didn't you insist on wearing a life jacket?' he snarled.

He could see his sudden attack had startled her and that she was floundering over how to answer him.

'That was my fault, Leo,' Tom answered like a protective beau. 'I said she wouldn't need one.'

'Excuse me. If I could just see the patient.' The doctor pushed the two men aside and crouched beside Lexi and Leo paced away from them before he did hit Tom. He hadn't been in a fist fight for seventeen years and he was disgusted with his loss of control that nearly saw him in one now. He didn't understand this possessive urge he felt towards Lexi Somers but it had to stop. She wasn't his and she never would be. He would never want her to be, despite his continued desire to take her to bed. That was just lust. Unusual in its intensity, yes, but still something he could control.

The doctor finished examining her and sat back on his haunches. 'You're fine. You've taken in a bit of water but your lungs sound clear enough. It doesn't appear you were hit and I expect you'll make a full recovery by this evening, but get some rest when you get back all the same.'

'I feel fine now,' Lexi said, hugging her knees close to her chest.

'Thanks, Gerard,' Leo murmured. 'Tom can return you to the yacht.'

Tom hesitated. 'I'm really sorry, Lexi.'

'That's okay, Tom. Accidents happen.'

'No, they don't,' Leo cut in. 'That was a stupid thing to do, Shepherd, and if I see you on one of my skis again without a life jacket I'll find someone else to do the East India project.'

Lexi's eyes flew to Leo as he squared off against Tom. The East India project was *his* idea? Lexi was shocked. The man worked tirelessly to save men he had probably never met after a building accident, knew the name of a staff member who ranked low down on the yacht's employment hierarchy, and now funded documentaries to bring the plight of children in the Third World to the attention of others—and these were just things she knew about. It didn't make sense that a man like that would not want to have a relationship with his son.

Unless he was still pining for the mother of that child?

Lexi's throat constricted at the unexpected thought that Leo might still be so in love with the beautiful Amanda Weston that he couldn't even stand to have their son in his orbit if he couldn't have her as well. Not that he'd said as much—but what other explanation could there be?

Lexi remembered how her own mother had been so deeply affected when her father's double life had come to light she had never risked her heart on another man again, turning instead to fostering children to fulfil the void his defection had left behind. Lexi had admired her mother for providing such a caring environment for other children, but she had always struggled when a child who had become part of their family had been returned to their own home.

'Okay, okay, my friend; I can see you're upset.' Tom held his hands up towards Leo in a conciliatory nature. 'We'll talk later by which time I hope your ire has cooled enough to accept my most humble apology.'

Lexi was surprised at Leo's aggressiveness and felt sorry for the retreating Tom. It had been remiss of him not to remind her to wear a life jacket but...

'Leo, really...it was an accident,' Lexi protested.

'It was avoidable.' Leo turned to face her, his blue eyes rapier sharp as he glared at her. 'If you had been wearing a life jacket you wouldn't have gone under,' he rasped forcefully.

'I didn't know I had to.' Was this really the same man who not twenty minutes ago had kissed her into a liquid puddle of need?

'I know that,' he snapped. 'And you know the reason Shepherd didn't tell you to put one on.'

His icy gaze raked down over her body and it took her a

second for his meaning to register. 'Are you suggesting…? That's ridiculous,' she said indignantly.

'It's the truth. He probably took his cue from your flirting with him during lunch. Probably earlier in the pool, for all I know.'

Lexi felt a blast of anger curl her hands into fists. 'And I suppose that kiss before on the sand was my fault as well? I encouraged you by lying back, unable to catch my breath.'

Leo rubbed the back of his neck. 'That kiss was the result of an extremely stressful situation,' he grated.

'Do tell.'

'Do tell what? As I recall, you weren't exactly reluctant a few minutes ago.'

Lexi shut up then. He was right; she'd been far from reluctant and she needed more time to reconcile her attraction to a man she didn't respect and who confused her mind and her senses in equal measure. She still felt light-headed from his kiss and the heat of his body pressing her so firmly into the sand.

'Yes, well, as you said, it was stress. And I think we should just forget it ever happened.'

'Fine with me.'

Lexi felt lost for words at his easy acceptance of her rebuttal and leant forward to brush the sugar-soft sand from her legs. What had she wanted him to say? That his kisses had been special? As if.

'We should get back,' he bit out tersely.

'Yes,' she agreed absently, too caught up in her own tumultuous response to this man to wonder at his irritation.

Leo led the way down to the water's edge and it wasn't until the hot sand gave way to the coolness of the water that she realised just *how* she would be getting back to the yacht.

'I'm not riding with you on that,' she protested a little too vehemently.

Leo waded towards the jet ski. 'What are you going to do—swim?'

He swung himself up onto the bobbing ski with envious athleticism, his leanly muscled torso rippling beneath his still damp shirt from where he'd held her wet body against him. 'It's not that far,' she said, trying to calculate the distance between the island and his yacht.

'It's over two kilometres and you've had a fall.'

'I was only winded,' she reminded him.

Leo gunned the engine and stretched out his hand. 'Get on,' he snarled, not bothering to hide his annoyance.

'You've ruined your trousers,' she commented inanely, noticing for the first time that he was still wearing suit trousers that were wet up to his knees and moulded to his muscular calves.

'My trousers are the least of my concerns,' he dismissed, beckoning to her. 'Come. You need to get out of this hot sun.'

Lexi eyed the jet ski dubiously. 'Can't you call the tender?'

'What with?' His lips curved into a mocking smile. 'My bat phone?'

Lexi didn't know if he was being humorous or not, she just knew that touching him was a bad idea. She fiddled with her necklace and his eyes narrowed on the movement.

'Don't make me have to come over there and get you,' he warned softly.

Lexi's heart skipped a beat, images of him lifting her up with those muscular arms and cradling her against his solid chest motivating her to wade through the warm water towards him. There was plenty of room behind him anyway and if he went slowly enough she wouldn't even have to hang onto him.

'Promise you won't go fast.'

'Whatever you want,' he drawled and Lexi's eyes cut to his. Whatever she wanted. She wanted him to kiss her like he had on the beach and never stop.

No.

She blinked away the unwelcome thoughts—that was so not what she wanted. Tomorrow she would be back in London and this weekend would be a distant dream. A one-night stand with a Russian playboy with questionable morals was not what the good doctor had ordered at all!

She reached out to take his hand and could have kicked herself for not grabbing the side of the ski instead when he effortlessly hauled her up in front of him, his strong thighs moulded to the outside of her own.

Lexi sucked in a quick breath. 'I can ride behind.'

'No,' his deep voice rumbled beside her ear and Lexi held herself completely still.

'And you dare to call me obstinate,' she fumed, so tense she felt ready to snap.

'Just sit still,' he growled as he expertly turned the machine towards the yacht and revved the engine.

Lexi ignored the way her insides clenched and turned molten with desire at his rough command. She held herself stiffly within the cage his arms made around her and only dared breathe again when he pulled up alongside the yacht's rear ramp.

A small welcoming committee was waiting to make sure she was okay and they clapped as Leo jumped easily onto the end of the yacht and held out his hand to help her up.

Lexi smiled up at everyone and then placed her hand in Leo's. The muscles in his forearms rippled as he effortlessly hauled her up and it was only as their eyes met that Lexi realised that she hadn't thanked him for rescuing her.

'Thank you,' she said, her voice husky and a little embarrassed.

She saw Leo's nostrils flare but other than that he didn't acknowledge her words and she turned her glazed eyes from his piercing gaze to focus on the others.

She reassured everyone that she was fine, mini drama over, and patted Tom's arm. 'Stop with the guilty look. I'm fine.'

'I can't help feeling bad. Let me take you up and get you a cool drink.'

She was about to say she'd like that when Leo interrupted, 'The doctor ordered rest.'

Lexi turned to find Leo glowering at Tom. 'I can—'

'Go to your room,' he said, his eyes on Tom.

Lexi felt her hackles rise at his proprietorial air. 'I'm fine,' she asserted.

He swung his blue eyes to hers and Lexi had to force herself not to feel intimidated. 'Good to know.' He stepped between her and Tom. 'One thing, angel.' He leaned close and lowered his tone so only she could hear and Lexi sucked in her breath to ensure that they didn't touch. 'If you're going to be having sex with anyone this weekend it won't be Tom Shepherd.'

Lexi blinked and before her befuddled brain could formulate any sort of decent response he had stalked past her and taken the curved staircase up to the next level, two steps at a time.

CHAPTER EIGHT

What on earth had he meant by that?

Lexi had asked herself the same question over and over all afternoon. She wasn't planning to have sex with anyone that weekend, let alone Tom Shepherd. And Leo's comment had been insulting in the extreme, implying that she was inviting attention, which she most definitely wasn't.

And if she wasn't going to have sex with Tom, then who was he thinking would take his place? Certainly not him if the way he'd jumped on her request that they forget all about those scorching kisses back on the beach was any indication.

Lexi leaned towards her bathroom mirror and swiped bronze eye shadow across her eyelids and then rubbed at the corner of her eye when she applied too much.

To say that Leo's behaviour confused her would be an understatement. Anyone would think that his behaviour towards her after the accident was possessive but, really, he was probably just concerned she was going to slap him with a law suit.

Deciding on a soft pink lip gloss, she stood back from the mirror and eyed herself critically. Her figure was neat and small and entirely unremarkable, although she did like the way her breasts looked in the halter-style amber maxi-dress she had bought in the sales last year and hadn't had a chance to wear yet. At least it made her look as if she had cleavage.

Shoving it into her weekend bag while Leo had prowled

around her living room while she packed had been a spur of the moment decision but now she wondered if it wasn't a little risqué. Not that she had anything else suitable to wear to his soirée tonight. A soirée she didn't even want to attend but had been informed she was expected to. And why was that? And why was her heart beating faster at the thought?

She stretched the silky fabric of her dress over her breasts, which suddenly seemed heavy and overly sensitive as they chafed the soft fabric. She traced her hands along the outer swell of each breast, remembering how Leo's much larger ones had skimmed that exact place hours earlier and her nipples tightened into aching points. A light thrumming feeling took up residence between her thighs as she imagined his mouth at her breast, his tongue. She imagined him taking her flesh into his mouth, could almost see the back of his blond head as she gazed at herself in the mirror.

A small whimper escaped from her lips and Lexi dropped her hands, her eyes slightly dazed as she gazed at her reflection. This was ridiculous. The man turned on the entire female population. Was she really considering adding herself to their ranks? Knowing the type of man he was? And, worse, knowing he would undoubtedly be disappointed with her sexually—as Brandon had been?

Oh, why was she even thinking like this?

She viciously twisted her heavy mass of hair into a bun and started stabbing pins into it.

A man who could have anyone did not go for moderately pretty girls unless they threw themselves at him and that was about as likely to happen as her being asked to model in a Victoria's Secret parade!

Lexi glanced down and realised she had used up the whole board of hairpins. Disgusted at her distracted thoughts, she stepped into high-heeled sandals and went to check on Ty.

Once she'd done that, she arrived in a ballroom the size of a basketball court, dimly lit by crystal chandeliers and alive with the happy chatter of Leo's guests and a live jazz band set up in the corner beside a wooden dance floor.

She swept her gaze around the room and her heart stopped beating when she noticed that Katya had taken up residence by Leo's side and it would have taken a crowbar to prise her away from him.

And he didn't seem to mind at all. In fact he was welcoming her attentions, his hand laying across the small of her back whenever she leaned in to whisper something to him—which appeared to be every five seconds.

Lexi's breath caught as her eyes drifted over Leo in a sleekly tailored black tuxedo. The black bow tie—which she had always found a touch effeminate on other men—only served to enhance his dangerous appeal—drawing attention to the strong column of his tanned neck and square jaw. The jacket hugged wide shoulders and drew in around his lean, hard-packed waist.

The tall model, dressed in a tiny white dress that loved every one of her generous curves and set off her red-gold hair, which hung like a smooth sheet down her back, the perfect feminine foil for his masculine sensuality. The yin to his yang.

Lexi drew in a sharp breath and tried to convince herself that she wasn't upset. Because he really wasn't her type and yet she literally ached to have him touch her again. To touch him. She could explain it away when she had been half asleep, or half-drowned, but now, in a room full of party-goers, his effect on her was a little hard to fob off.

Not wanting to dwell on something she couldn't fully understand, she startled a waiter by whisking a glass of champagne off his tray as he walked past. Not that she knew why she bothered because she doubted she'd be able to get a millimetre of the delicious liquid past the boulder lodged in her throat.

She felt her breathing take on an uneven kilter and her

heart pound and for a minute she felt lost and completely humiliated. Because, even though she had taken umbrage with Leo's kisses, with his possessive behaviour in front of Tom, a small part of her had thought that…what? That he might actually want to be with her? That he might seriously find her attractive? That he might have invited her to his party to be with him?

She felt like a fool. A fool who had dressed up for nothing.

No, not nothing. She would have a good time if it killed her.

'Care to dance, *omorphe kopella*?'

Lexi turned at the sound of a deep Mediterranean voice beside her. The man who had spoken to her was tall, though not as tall as Leo, and clean-shaven, with raven black hair and a cleft in his chin.

'My name is Anton Pompidou. I am a lawyer with the Greek government.'

'I'm Lexi Somers. Childcare manager.'

He smiled and held out his hand. 'You forgot to say beautiful.' His smile wasn't exactly smarmy, but he was smooth and she could tell he was used to getting his way with women. Lexi was just about to decline his invitation when she noticed Leo place his hand in the small of Katya's back again as she leaned in to whisper some sweet nothing in his ear and found herself agreeing instead. 'I'd love to.'

Anton's smile widened and Lexi fervently hoped he didn't read too much into her overzealous acceptance.

Which, a short time later, after he offered to escort her outside for some 'fresh air', she realised he had.

'Look, I'm really sorry,' she informed him as he tried to take her into his arms, 'but I really did just come out here for air.'

'Is there a problem out here?'

Lexi made a small, pained noise as she recognised Leo's gravelly accented voice behind her just before he came into view.

'No problem, Mr Aleksandrov.' The tall Greek released her and all but bowed down to him. 'Miss Somers required some fresh air.'

'And now she requires some privacy,' Leo drawled, his eyes pinned to hers as he spoke to the lawyer.

Some small part of Lexi willed the man to defy him but it didn't happen. Leo had an air of command about him few men possessed and even fewer argued with.

'You should know that when a man offers to take a woman outside for air it's rarely what he's offering,' he said shortly.

Lexi turned back to the twinkling lights of the distant island she had been admiring earlier. 'Thanks for the tip.'

'That is Naxos,' he told her after a brief pause.

'I didn't ask.'

'You are angry with me.'

Lexi released a deep breath and turned her head to look at him. She thought how unfairly good-looking he was in the moonlight. 'He thinks we're together now.'

'So?'

'So…so you're overbearing and arrogant.'

'So?'

Lexi huffed out a breath. 'I don't know. Just go back to your supermodel accessory, would you. I'm too tired to argue with you tonight.' She turned back to look out over the inky sea that shone silver in the moonlight.

'Then don't.'

Lexi's eyes swung back to his and she shook her head as she clearly read the meaning behind that simple statement. 'You can't just waltz out here and treat me as if…as if…'

'As if I own you?'

His silky words stole the breath from her lungs and set her heart pumping madly behind her breastbone. 'What do you want, Leo?' she asked without really meaning to but now waiting with bated breath for his answer.

* * *

You.

The single word floated into the front of his brain like a neon sign and he didn't try to push it away as usual.

Why bother? He wanted her. She wanted him and he had already decided the best thing to do now was to give in to it.

He'd tried to ignore her all night. Had even used Katya as some sort of shield, but as soon as Anton Pompidou had laid his hands on Lexi he'd known the game was up.

Warning bells might be going off inside his head louder than a New Year's Eve countdown but he might as well have been in a kamikaze jet on autopilot for all the good they were doing him.

He looked at her now, her low-cut gown shimmering around her, and he knew that he wanted her more than he'd wanted to possess anything else in his life.

'You,' he said softly, the word falling between them like a sacred offering.

He heard her breath hitch and saw her body tense, her nipples tight as they pushed against the silky fabric of her dress. He knew the air was still too warm to have brought about that reaction and his groin hardened to painful proportions as it read the signals her body was sending out.

If he didn't touch her soon, if he didn't get her beneath him in his bed, he just might implode.

She wasn't looking at him but awareness vibrated between them and burned up some of the few remaining brain cells that were still functioning inside his head.

Then she turned her head, an errant curl falling over her forehead, the look in her eyes utterly disparaging.

'Why? Did your supermodel turn you down?'

He sucked in a steadying breath. 'I didn't offer her anything.'

'Really?' She arched a delicate brow and snagged the piece of hair behind her ear. 'Could have fooled me.'

'I think I hurt you tonight.'

'You confuse me,' she said with raw honesty, 'but if you're seriously offering me a night in your bed then I have to tell you I'm not interested in casual sex.'

Leo studied her, aware of the scent of the sea air and the loud thud of his own heart.

'There will be nothing casual about the sex we have, angel.'

Her eyes dropped away from his and he wondered at the flash of—uncertainty? Insecurity?—that crossed her face.

'Lexi?'

She shook her head at him. 'I've known men like you and… you have too many secrets, Leo. I couldn't be with someone I couldn't trust.'

Leo felt the skin on his face pull tight. 'Are you saying I'm dishonest?'

'I'm saying I don't know who you are. You give nothing away and…'

'Somebody hurt you?'

Lexi huffed out a breath and shrugged her shoulders but the movement was stilted. 'My father led a double life and when my mother found out it nearly killed her.' She tugged at the necklace nestled between her breasts agitatedly and then dropped it when she saw him looking. 'I don't know why I just told you that.'

'Because you want to sleep with me but you're torn.'

She shook her head. Oh, to be so confident. 'I've never met anyone like you but…like I said, you have secrets and they scare me.'

'Believe me, *moya milaya*, it would scare you more to know them.'

She shivered and wrapped her arms around her waist and Leo cursed himself for saying what he had. Then he cursed her for being the person she was. She was too genuine and almost innocent in her view of the world. She made his conscience spike and he knew that pursuing her after this would be selfish and he'd promised himself he'd never be selfish again after Sasha's death.

He heard a discreet cough behind him. 'Someone had better be dead, Danny,' he growled, not looking at his EA.

'You might wish that were the case in a minute.'

Leo turned at the serious note in Danny's voice. 'What is it?'

'You said to inform you immediately if we got word from Amanda.'

Leo's eyes narrowed. 'You found her, then.'

'Not exactly. I've been checking your emails all day and this came in.' He handed him a piece of paper and Leo took it, a sense of dread forming a knot in his belly.

He scanned the email and started sweating like a man trapped in a steel cage with a dozen hungry lions for company. 'Married?' He shook his head. 'She can't do this.'

Danny didn't say anything and Leo knew that his worst nightmare had come true. Amanda was demanding that he take full custody of Ty. She had remarried and Ty didn't fit into their lifestyle.

He felt the fist in his belly rise to his heart and emotion and pain clawed at him as memories of the past hurtled into his consciousness.

Air became choked in his lungs and Leo felt the panic he had experienced at the childcare centre when he'd first seen Ty take hold.

He needed space.

Time to think. Without looking at either occupant on the deck, he crumpled the piece of paper into his fist and stalked off.

CHAPTER NINE

LEXI wandered down the long walkways and spiral staircases until she came to her and Ty's suite of rooms. She checked on Ty and smoothed his hair off his forehead as she watched him sleeping peacefully. He looked so much like Leo and her mind automatically wondered where he had gone. What he was doing.

He had said 'married' in such a tortured voice Lexi could only surmise that Amanda had remarried and the news had clearly devastated him. Her heart clenched in reaction and her skin grew hot. Her earlier assumption that he still harboured strong feelings for Amanda Weston was clearly correct.

She straightened Ty's sheets and let herself out of his room and crossed to her own. She knew Carolina was asleep in the other room with the monitor on and that she would not be needed any more tonight.

She kicked off her heels and wandered out onto her private terrace. The air held a faint chill now that a soft breeze had picked up and she rubbed her bare arms. She turned back inside and poured herself a glass of water and sat down at the small writing desk, running her fingers over the edge of her laptop before jumping up again. She was too wired to sleep and too restless to work.

Again her mind drifted to Leo and she wondered if he would want someone to be there for him when he was feeling terrible. Instinctively, she knew that he wouldn't but some-times people didn't know what they needed until they had it. She knew he wasn't a talker but maybe he'd never had anyone offer a listening ear before. She might question his morals and his life choices, but he was a human being in pain and everyone needed someone at a time like this.

Not questioning her motives too closely, Lexi donned her heels and decided that the only way to put her mind at rest was to find him, make sure he was okay and then return to her room.

Pleased with her plan, she took the elevator up to his level and tapped lightly on his door. After a minute she knocked harder and then, still hearing nothing, turned the door knob and opened the door.

She hadn't really expected it to be unlocked and now she was faced with the dilemma of whether to just close it and leave or…close it definitely!

'Remind me to station security outside my door.' Leo's gruff words carried across the room and nearly gave her a heart attack and Lexi let the door swing further open, just in time to see Leo disappearing into the opposite doorway.

Okay, so he wasn't dead… Lexi let her gaze drift over the room in front of her and gasped at the size and understated opulence that greeted her eyes.

It was a living room with a huge cream sofa and match-ing chairs that looked comfortable enough to sleep on. Large domed lamps flanked the sofa and gave the room an intimate, golden glow that set off the smooth polished cabinetry around the room to perfection. A flat-screen TV lined one entire wall and opposite that an open doorway led into what Lexi assumed was the bedroom Leo had just disappeared through.

Before she could stop herself she crossed the carpeted floor, trying not to think about the last time she had entered Leo's bedroom in his London apartment, and peeked inside. It *was* his bedroom and it was dominated by a huge bed facing curved floor-to-ceiling windows that looked onto a private deck. Clearly the man liked his views.

Lexi saw him sprawled on one of the sun loungers outside and wandered to the open doorway; the light of the moon casting him in shadows.

'What do you want?'

He didn't turn and Lexi hovered there, uncertain as to whether she should stay or go, some inner instinct telling her that he needed her right now. 'I wanted to make sure you were okay.'

Stars twinkled overhead in the navy sky and the only sound was that of water slapping as it broke against the side of the yacht. 'Still trying to solve the problems of the world, angel?'

Lexi returned her gaze back to him. He wasn't looking at her, but lay with his eyes closed and his hands folded behind his head. 'No. I thought you might like company.'

He opened his eyes, his gaze raking her from head to toe before closing them again. 'You're wearing too many clothes for the company I need right now.'

'It might help if you talked about what's wrong.'

'Really.' His voice was snide and Lexi questioned her decision to interrupt him. 'Let's give it a try, shall we. I don't want Amanda to be married and to leave me in charge of the care of my son.' He bared his teeth in a parody of a smile. '*Net*. Still married. What a surprise.'

Lexi moved out onto the balcony and shivered as she felt the chill in the air descend on her bare skin. Or was that just the frost coming off the brooding man with his eyes now fixed on some dark spot in the distance? She perched on the matching chair beside his. 'I know you're upset at the news.'

'Upset? I'm not upset, angel. I'm furious.'

'Because you love her?' she acknowledged ruefully.

'You think that's what's going on here? You think that I *love* Amanda Weston?'

'You seemed devastated by the email she sent and—'

His sneer stopped the rest of her words. 'And you thought it was a love gone wrong. I don't do love, angel.'

'If it's not love you feel for Amanda, then…I'm confused. Why do you act as if Ty doesn't exist?'

'Because to me he doesn't.'

Lexi's breath caught in her throat. She wouldn't believe that. She *couldn't*. 'I don't believe you.'

He paused and she didn't think he was going to answer her.

'You want to know what happened with Amanda, I'll tell you. She came onto me at the Brussels Airport when all flights were grounded and we had sex. It was never going to be anything more than one night but she was looking for a rich husband and we used her condom—which I later found out she had already tampered with. It was a one-night fluke but she hit the jackpot.'

'That's terrible.'

Leo looked at Lexi's shocked face. Why had he told her that? He'd never told anyone before. Was it because he was sick of her thinking that he'd abandoned Ty for nothing? 'Poor Lexi. Doesn't that fit in with your ideal world where two parents love their children beyond measure?' He shook his head dourly and turned back to the ocean.

'I don't live in a fantasy world, Leo, if that's what you're suggesting. I know that sometimes one loving parent is better than two who can't get along.'

Leo glanced back at her averted face. Her chin was angled defiantly, her spine rigid. He knew instantly that whatever had gone on in her own childhood had affected her deeply and, despite his never having been interested in a woman's past before, he couldn't hold back his curiosity. 'You're talking about your father's double life, I take it.'

She stared at her hands for a minute and then her eyes met his. 'Yes. My father was a mildly successful golfer who travelled the world and my mother accepted that as part and parcel of loving him. She was a very understanding person and she never pushed to travel with him—mainly, I think, because she would have found it hard with Joe and I—but nor did she push to marry him. Then one night her world fell apart when the daughter he had fathered with his long-time mistress had an accident and his mistress gave him an ultimatum. Mum or her.'

Leo looked over and saw that Lexi's jaw was tight. 'And he chose the other woman.'

'He did try to visit Joe and I but…somehow he never seemed to make it.' She gave a forced laugh. 'For years we would dutifully dress in our best clothes once a month in the hope that today would be the day he would keep to his promise. Only it rarely was and soon Joe stopped dressing up altogether.'

'And you?' he asked. 'Did you stop dressing up?'

She fingered the necklace, a move he had noticed her do countless times before when she was nervous, and wondered who had given it to her. 'I'm a bit of an optimist.' She laughed a little self-consciously. 'I might have given him more of a chance than Joe.'

'A bit of a dreamer, you mean,' he said, but there was no harshness behind the words. Just resignation that he could never be as forgiving. 'Who gave you that?'

His eyes dropped to the necklace she was drawing back and forth across her bottom lip and wished it was his tongue.

'My father gave it to me on my tenth birthday.'

'And you've never taken it off since,' he guessed.

She let it drop back down between her breasts and when she spoke her voice was choked. 'You make me sound pathetic.'

'Not pathetic. Just someone who believes in happy ever afters.'

'Is that such a bad thing?'

Leo wasn't particularly comfortable with the turn of the

conversation and contemplated telling her to leave. If only he didn't want her so damned much. 'Only if it means you don't see things for what they really are,' he said, raising a mocking eyebrow, willing her to deny that she didn't.

'What makes you think that I don't?'

His eyebrow climbed higher. 'You wear a necklace to keep a connection with a man who deserted you and you need to ask that?'

Lexi's hand rose to her neck. 'I just… I never…'

'You never wanted to accept that he chose the other family?'

Her hand dropped and she pushed off the lounger and walked to the railing, gripping it firmly and leaning slightly forward as she gazed down at the sea. 'You're very astute.'

Leo didn't respond. He could see that she was deep in thought and he was struggling with his own desire to go to her. Comfort her. Then she glanced back over her shoulder and the delicate muscles around her shoulder blades shifted alluringly.

'Children are innocent. They don't ask to be born. They deserve proper care. And…' she paused and he watched her throat work as she swallowed '…I guess I always hoped he'd come back. I hated that his selfishness caused my mother to have to work two jobs, because that was hard on us all.' She paused. 'I don't know why I still wear the necklace.'

'So you became a childcare worker to provide care for kids whose parents have to go to work?'

She looked surprised, as if she hadn't made that connection before. But it explained why she was so keen for him to have a relationship with Ty and why she was so wary of him. A wariness she was right to feel.

'What's your relationship with your father like now?' he asked softly.

'We don't have one.' Her eyes connected earnestly with his. 'It's what I've been trying to tell you. Now is the time to get to know Ty. I haven't seen my father in ten years and Joe even longer than that.'

Leo looked away as she came to sit back down opposite him. He had more than just Amanda's subterfuge keeping him away from Ty.

'You should be thankful he left, angel. Sometimes a man who is forced to marry because he gets a woman pregnant makes everyone's life hell.'

She looked at him curiously. 'That sounds like you're speaking from experience.'

Leo didn't know if it was the lateness of the hour, the shock of Amanda's defection or Lexi Somers soft compassion but he found himself wanting to tell her things he'd never told another living soul.

He sighed. Maybe if he did tell her some of it she would understand why Ty was better off without him. 'My father married my mother because she was pregnant with me and he spent the first ten years of my life making it a living hell.'

Lexi looked at the taut lines of Leo's neck and knew he was speaking the truth, but it was a long way from what she'd read about him. 'I thought you had a happy childhood?'

'Ah, my bio. Nice story, isn't it.'

'What's the real story?' she asked quietly.

'Why do you want to know? Hoping to earn a few extra dollars by selling an exposé?'

'Of course not. I just want to help.'

'Like I said. You have too many clothes on for that. Not that I don't love that dress. You know what it makes me want to do?' He swung his legs to the side and twisted in his seat so that he was facing her, his knees wide, his feet firmly planted either side of her legs. 'It makes me want to grab those two triangles of fabric barely covering your gorgeous breasts and rip it straight down the middle. Does that shock you, little

Lexi?' He paused and all Lexi could hear was the sound of her own heart beating too fast. 'Or excite you?'

She knew he was trying to distract her. That he didn't want to talk about his life story. She also knew that she wanted him to tell her. She wanted to know him. Know the real Leo Aleksandrov. As if seeking to put distance between them, he moved abruptly to stand at the railing, staring off into the balmy distance.

Lexi moistened her lips before asking, 'What's the real story, Leo?'

He turned his head and looked down at her. 'Like horror stories do you?' His voice was a low growl and Lexi sensed the pain he was trying desperately to hold at bay.

He had the look of a lost child about him and Lexi was reminded of Ty the first time she had met him, mistrust stamped all over his beautiful face. But she wouldn't push Leo any further. It would be beyond arrogant of her to assume that just because she found it better to talk through her issues, he would too.

He rubbed a hand over the back of his neck and for a minute she didn't think he was going to say anything. Then he flopped back down on the chair and stared at the starry sky. 'I grew up in the Tundra—a hellhole of a place where nothing grows and it's so bitterly cold in winter you feel like your bones are freezing. My father was a miner with Mafioso connections and my mother was a shop girl who let love turn her blind. When my father drank he turned violent and my mother bore the brunt of his loss of control. At times I tried to stop him but I could never protect her from his brute strength.'

'How could you—you were just a child?' she cried.

'No child wants to see their mother hurt. Of course every time I tried to help he thought it was a great joke and tried to challenge me. Taunted me until I gave in.'

Lexi felt sick and it took a great deal of effort to control the emotion in her voice. 'How old were you when this started?'

'Six, seven. I don't remember.' He gave a telling shrug.

He remembered all right. Too well, Lexi guessed.

'I do remember his favourite modus operandi was a sly backhand just when you thought the jibes and beltings had finished.'

Lexi swallowed and made an inarticulate sound of distress. 'Do you still see him?' she asked, her breathing ragged and uneven where his was almost meditatively calm.

'No.' His eyes when they fixed on hers were empty. 'He died in prison.'

'Was that when you were ten?'

He looked at her warily.

'You said the first ten years were awful. I just wondered if that was when your father went to jail.'

'Got a sharp brain, haven't you, angel?'

'So…things got better after that?'

'Things did get better. My father went to prison and I went to live with my uncle.'

'Where was your mother?'

'She couldn't look after me. I was too wild. Used to get into fights all the time. Very bad news.'

Lexi was still trying to comprehend that his mother had sent him away when she noticed that his tone had darkened. 'Your mother sent you away?'

'Oh, Lexi, with the bleeding heart. Don't be so outraged.' He touched her face briefly and then stood up and paced across the balcony, unable to keep still. 'She had her reasons and it was the best decision she could have made. My uncle wasn't at all like my father. He was gruff and proud, but he controlled his emotions. Until I came to stay, he had lived his adult life alone. He taught me how to contain my rage.'

Lexi wondered if Leo realised that he had made himself over in his uncle's image. A man facing the world alone. Her heart went out to him. 'Do you still see him?'

'He died. A work-related accident.'

'On a building site,' Lexi guessed.

'*Da*. And now you know.' He spread his arms wide. 'All the dirty details of who I really am and why I can't be a father to Ty.'

'No—' Lexi shook her head '—I don't know that at all.'

He huffed out a laugh. 'Then you're not as smart as I thought you were. I'm not a good bet, Lexi. I can't be responsible for Ty.'

Was that it? Was that why he was so determined that Ty was better off without him? Not because he was afraid of losing his lifestyle, but because he was afraid of becoming his father. Afraid of hurting those who relied on him.

'Leo, that's fear talking. It's not who you are,' she said, catching her breath at his fierce expression as he swung around to face her again.

'Haven't you heard anything I've said? I'm a violent man.'

'You think you'd hurt Ty?' Lexi shook her head. 'I don't.'

'My father couldn't help it. Who's to say I'll be any different?'

'Your father *could* help it. He *chose* not to.'

Lexi's heart went out to Leo trapped as a young child in a world with such a damaged adult, but she forced herself to focus on what still needed to be said.

'Leo, I don't know who your parents were but I'd say they were two people who shouldn't have been together. They brought out the worst in each other and maybe didn't have the maturity to see the error of their ways. But whatever their story is—it doesn't have to be yours.'

'It doesn't matter, Lexi. I'm empty inside. I have nothing to give.'

Lexi frowned. 'You think you can't love?' How much this man had suffered!

'Not think. I don't.'

'What about your uncle?'

'Yes, maybe. I cared for him. But...' His voice trailed away and he rubbed the back of his neck. 'There's no point talking about this.'

'Because it hurts too much?'

'Because I am what I am.'

Leo gripped the railing more tightly and Lexi went to him and laid her hand on his arm. 'Spend time with Ty. Just the two of you. I haven't seen you take any time off since we got here.'

'No.' He moved his hand out from under hers and flopped down on the sun lounger, his hands dangling between his wide-spread knees.

Lexi could feel him closing off and she didn't know what else to say to him. 'He needs you, Leo.'

'He needs a decent father.'

Lexi placed her hands on her hips, determined to get through to him on this point. 'Yes. You. And you need him.'

He shook his head slowly and the look in his eyes as they swept over her changed, became heated. 'What I need is for you to go to bed.'

'I—'

He shook his head, his eyes becoming guarded. 'No more. There's only so much happy reminiscing a man can take. Especially when the woman he's reminiscing with is only half dressed.' His lips twisted into a wry smile.

'I'm not half dressed.'

'Tell me you're wearing a bra beneath that dress.'

'Well, no, but—'

'Like I said. Half dressed.'

She sensed the air thicken between them and couldn't look away. It was like being on the beach again, just before he'd kissed her. His blue eyes dark, his features taut, but not with pain now—with something her body instantly recognised. And wanted.

'I think you're trying to change the subject.'

'Smart *and* quick.'

He stared at her. Lexi became aware that the only sound on the balcony was the beating of her own frantic heart. She couldn't have moved even if she'd wanted to and he recognised her hesitation for what it was.

He shook his head slowly. 'You don't do casual sex.' His voice was heavy, low, laden with sensual restraint.

Lexi swallowed. Kissing him had shaken her to her core. As had his revelations. He was right. She didn't do casual sex. Or at least she never had before, but would indulging in it once be so wrong? She wasn't deluding herself that sex with Leo would be more than that. But he made her feel things she'd never felt before. She couldn't help wanting more of that. But could she risk her self-esteem on it?

She stared at him. He looked predatory. Hungry. For her?

Her nipples tingled and a hollow aching feeling made her lower body clench. With sudden alarm Lexi realised that her body was already readying itself to make love with him. Just the thought made the throbbing worse and her heart kicked up. It seemed, from her body's point of view, she couldn't *not* risk it. 'You said the sex wouldn't be casual.' Was that breathless, seductive voice really hers?

He didn't respond immediately and she was momentarily struck with the horrible sense that maybe he had been trying to let her down gently.

Like a helpless mouse that had backed itself into a corner, Lexi's stomach pitched and then he held out his hand.

'Come here.'

CHAPTER TEN

LEXI noted the way his chest moved in time with his deep even breaths and that the skin on his face seemed to be pulled tight. His eyes tracked over her with such sexual purpose there was no mistaking his intention and her arousal returned on a rush of liquid heat.

He wanted her and she wanted him and nothing else seemed to matter right now.

As if in a dream state, she moved towards him.

When she reached him he widened his legs and drew her closer between his thighs, his large hands light as they enveloped her waist.

Then he breathed deeply and rested his forehead on her chest.

Lexi could feel the warmth of his breath through the thin fabric of her dress and gave in to the urge to stroke her fingers through his short hair. The strands felt crisp and soft at the same time. Her fingers flexed and clung and she wondered if the hair on his chest would feel the same way.

He raised his head and her hands stilled at the intensity of the desire she could see banked behind his eyes.

'Do you know how beautiful you are?'

No, but he made her *feel* beautiful. Lexi felt a shiver race through her whole body and she knew he felt it because his fingers tightened around her waist. And thank God they did because her bones melted and her legs nearly gave out.

Her hands moved of their own accord down the side of his face and cupped his square jaw, her fingertips scraping over the stubble on his face. 'I imagined this would be hard,' she murmured. 'But it's soft.'

She saw him take a deep breath. One of the hands at her waist rose to the nape of her neck as he gently guided her face down to his. 'I want you,' he said gruffly and another spasm of need weakened her knees even more and brought her closer to the heat of his big body.

She wanted him too. She couldn't deny it. Couldn't even remember why she should. Nothing seemed to matter except this man and this moment and then his lips finally touched hers and her brain closed down completely.

Leo's mouth already knew the shape and texture of her sweet mouth but still, kissing her now, was like the first time and his groin jerked with pleasure as her mouth opened over his. He tried to be gentle, but he was already hard and aching with desire for her. His tongue circling inside her mouth as he tasted her. Hers following his lead and tasting him right back.

He smoothed his hands up over her naked back and then he wrapped them around her and stood up, taking her with him.

She gasped and wrapped her arms around his neck as he carried her inside and he felt like a warrior who had just won a great prize.

He set her down beside his bed and stood her before him as he sat on the edge of it. His eyes drifted over her gorgeous body and, wanting to see all of her at once, he gripped the silky fabric covering her breasts and would have ripped the dress in two if she hadn't put her hands over his to stop him. 'I love this dress.'

He smiled into her passion-drugged eyes. 'I don't have

time for zips. And I promise I'll buy twenty more for you to replace it.' Then he ripped it—straight down the middle.

Her breath hitched in her throat and her hands immediately came up to cover her breasts.

Leo felt her shocked hesitation and glanced into her eyes. 'What is it, angel?'

Her mouth pulled down at the corners. 'I'm afraid I'm not what you're used to.'

She was self-conscious! The realisation floored him and reminded him of her hesitation on the upstairs deck. Uncertainty wasn't what he had expected from this woman who was verbally able to go toe to toe with him when no other woman had ever tried before.

Leo ran a finger along the defined bones of her clavicle and felt something reverent pass through him. He couldn't remember ever wanting a woman as much as he wanted Lexi Somers and his body was vibrating with the tension of holding himself in check.

He leaned back slowly so that he could take his fill of her. She stood before him like an elegant courtesan—her petite frame ghosted in the faint light from his bedside lamps, her hands covering her small, perfect breasts, her hair still up, but slightly messy, and a delicate lace bikini brief that rode low on her hips.

He breathed deeply and smoothed his hand up her neck and over the smooth skin of her jaw. 'You're the most beautiful woman I've ever seen,' he said huskily, realising how true that was, his hands not quite steady as he tunnelled them into her hair to hold her still to receive his deep kiss. His fingers met resistance and he tore his mouth from hers and started pulling hair pins from her hair. Within seconds his hands were filled with small brown pieces of looped metal and he leaned back and stared up at her. 'Remind me to take out shares in carbon steel the next time you shop for hair products.'

She laughed, a soft, sultry sound that curled inside him.

'My hair isn't that easy to work with,' she said, slowly raising her arms to loosen it so that it fell past her shoulders like a dark cloud.

Leo meant to dump the small pins on the bedside table beside her but, with her arms raised above her head and her body almost naked before him, he quite forgot to breathe, the pins falling to the carpet.

He reached out and measured the span of her waist with both hands. Then he smiled. 'So small, so feminine.' He leaned forward and planted open-mouth kisses on the outside of each rounded breast. Her body quivered and waited as he slowly made his way closer and closer to the tight pink buds that awaited his lips. She moaned softly and he felt her nails bite into his shoulders as she shifted slightly so that his mouth skated across her nipple. He blew gently and her hands moved to cradle his skull to guide him to her.

'Please, Leo,' she begged, arching closer.

'Please what?' he whispered against her. 'Please this?' He laved her nipple with the tip of his tongue and when she whimpered and sagged against him he held her up easily and suckled her more fully into his mouth. Her fingernails dug into his shoulder blades and gave him a heady feeling that made his erection throb.

'Take off my shirt,' he growled against her flesh, tearing the buttons as he helped her get it off him so that she could touch him in return.

His nostrils flared as her hands found his chest and her hungry caresses sent his self-control skittering into the ether.

She almost sobbed with pleasure as he tortured each breast in turn and he felt a primitive thrill at the feel of her pressing into him. She was every bit as responsive as he had imagined she would be and she was his. All his.

She made a moue of protest as he released her nipple. 'It only gets better from here, angel,' he promised throatily, not exactly gentle as he wrapped one arm around her waist and, bringing his mouth to hers, turned her and deposited her on the middle of the bed. He moved her legs apart with his knee, his aching body looming over hers as he continued to ravage her mouth.

He kept his weight on his arms as her hands swept over his biceps, his shoulders, and down the hard planes of his chest, setting him on fire wherever she touched him.

'Leo, it's too much.' Her lower body writhed against his knee and he could no longer wait to test the wet heat of her arousal. He trailed his hand down her flat belly and skimmed across the top of her panties, a rough sound escaping his throat as he palmed her and found her damp. Her hips came up off the bed and he released her breast to tug her panties off. He sat back on his haunches and gazed down at her femininity. Her splayed thighs, moist breasts and dark hair that was wild against the cream bedspread.

He settled his hand against her abdomen as he'd imagined doing many times before and moved one of her legs further apart.

'You're not naked yet,' she murmured and he could hear the embarrassment in her voice.

His eyes met hers. 'If I get naked I'll climb inside you and I want to make it last.' His thumbs pressed gently against the soft skin of her inner thighs.

'Leo…' His name was more a groan than a word. 'Come back up here.'

He glanced up at her. 'You don't like what I'm about to do?'

Her chest rose unsteadily as she drew in a deep breath. 'I don't know,' she muttered, shielding her eyes with her arm.

He paused. No man had done this for her? He felt a primitive thrill race through him at the thought of introducing her to such intimate pleasure.

'Look at me,' he commanded roughly, waiting for her to move her arm and then watching her face as he trailed a finger lightly through her silky moist curls, barely restraining himself as he gently parted her. Her breath hitched and his heart beat erratically.

'Beautiful,' he whispered, sliding a finger inside her. He had imagined her like this from the moment he'd laid eyes on her and the reality far outweighed his fantasy. He watched the way her eyes widened and her mouth went lax as he drove her higher and higher towards her climax. He was completely wild for her but, more than that, he wanted to watch her come. Wanted to taste her while she did. He'd never experienced such an intense desire to give a woman pleasure.

He watched her eyes open even wider as he lowered his head towards her body, his brain closing down as he slid his hands beneath her buttocks and raised her to his mouth for the first time.

Lexi's fingers tangled in Leo's short hair and she nearly screamed as she felt his tongue and his lips doing the most delicious things to her body. Brandon had never touched her like this and the pleasure was beyond her realm of comprehension. Her body felt as if it were a puppet moving closer and closer to something just outside of her reach. Then she heard Leo's voice from far away telling her to relax and when she did, she screamed, her body shattering into a million tiny pieces and emotions she'd never experienced spiralled through her.

For all she knew she could have lost hours as her body continued to shoot jolts of pleasure through her system and a satisfied smile curved her lips as she felt Leo rise up over her in a purely dominating posture.

'There were stars,' she murmured dazedly, her arms looping lethargically around his neck. 'And I don't think I'll ever move again.'

'Good. Because you're exactly where you need to be. And this time I might throw in the moon as well.' Leo's accent was rougher than ever.

'Promises, promises,' she teased, lying still as she felt him sheath himself with a condom.

Leo laughed and planted his palms either side of her face to protect her from his full weight and she could feel his hair-roughened thighs lying solidly between her own.

She felt the hard length of him probe her entrance and his biceps shook as he held himself in check. 'Open wider angel, and let me in.' She did as he commanded and his control seemed to give out because he surged into her in one power-ful thrust of his hips.

Lexi gasped and tensed as her body felt stretched like never before.

Leo stilled and dragged his lips from hers, his hands cra-dling her face. 'Lexi, are you okay?'

She sucked in a breath and nodded, her fingernails easing out of the dents she'd made in his hips.

'You're so tight, *moya milaya*. Just relax for me and we'll fit together perfectly.'

His words made Lexi's pelvis soften even more and when he felt her muscles release he sank all the way inside her. He held still for another moment but Lexi's body had already adjusted and he was hitting a spot that sent gushes of plea-sure cascading through her lower body. She raised one of her legs up over his hips and felt him smile against her mouth.

'That's better.' His mouth left a moist trail over her jawline and Lexi's body arched under his as he began to move inside her in a masterful rhythm. 'Now come for me again, angel, while I'm inside you,' he ordered in a voice that sounded as unsteady as she felt. Lexi couldn't resist the build-up of plea-sure any more than the tide could resist the pull of the moon. She couldn't think as her body shattered once more in an even deeper climax. Her body clamped down around his and drew a sound from his throat that was almost subhuman as he surged forward twice more before finding his own release.

* * *

Leo woke, slightly disoriented, and shifted under the weight of the warm, naked female who had wound herself around him like tinsel on a Christmas tree, one leg thrown over his thighs, her head nestled in the crook of his arm, her small breasts flattened against his side and her slender fingers spread wide over his chest. He didn't remember falling asleep but a glance at the faint grey dawn outside the windows told him he must have. The yacht was still moving so he knew they hadn't yet reached Athens.

He gently flexed his stiff shoulder muscles and Lexi adjusted herself like a contented cat, snuggling in closer and sighing in her sleep.

His fist clenched at the sound and he had the instant urge to break free from her hold and run for his life. He wasn't used to sleeping next to someone, that was the problem. It had nothing to do with the deep sense of well-being enveloping him in a warm, peaceful cocoon. A concept he hadn't felt in…forever.

It wasn't that he had a lot of one-night stands; it was more that he liked his space. Needed his space. And he didn't want any woman to get the wrong idea and start mentally rearranging his furniture.

His fingers drifted through the silk of Lexi's hair as he recalled in minute detail how he had taken that warm, tight body with his own. He felt his groin stir at the memory and knew that the smart thing to do would be to get out of bed and go for an early morning swim. Grab a coffee and start work.

Some of his tension must have leached out of him because Lexi whimpered and caressed his shoulder with her smooth cheek. Leo's hand immediately flexed against her hip and slid down around the soft curve of her lower back, his fingers stroking her soft skin. She must have liked it because the leg she had thrown over his thigh rubbed his and now he was fully erect and, instead of following his saner instincts and climbing out of bed, he found himself shifting again and urging her small, compact body to lie over his. Her thighs automatically splayed to accommodate his hardness while his two hands caressed her curvaceous bottom.

He shouldn't be doing this.

Taking advantage of her while she slept. He might have stopped but then she widened her thighs even more and whispered, 'Don't stop,' into his ear. Leo turned his head and caught her mouth with his in a kiss that went from soft to carnal faster than his Maserati hit a hundred clicks. She pushed up sleepily, her hands on his shoulders, her mane of hair falling around her and resting just above her pert breasts, which had taken on a luminescent quality in the pre-dawn light. Leo groaned and reached for one at the same time as he delved into his side drawer for protection. She arched into his caress and lifted her lower body against his but he stayed her with a hand on her hip.

'Wait,' he whispered gruffly.

He protected them both and nearly came on the spot as she reached down and guided him into her body.

Her moan precipitated his own and he'd never felt such overpowering pleasure as he did at that moment. If he'd been at all capable of thinking he might have been concerned but she moved her hips experimentally against his and he pushed her hair back off her breasts and cupped her in his large hands, watching as she rode him into the sweetest orgasm of his life.

While he was still coming down from a place he didn't think he'd ever been before he stroked a lazy line up and down her spine.

She made a low murmur of pleasure and slipped off him to snuggle into the crook of his arm again.

'I'm all sweaty.'

'You feel fantastic.' He traced a finger over her hip and the gentle swell of her belly without really realising he was doing it. Then she shifted her top leg more comfortably over his and his heart caught.

'You know, when I first saw you I thought you were heartless and unapproachable,' she murmured sleepily. 'But that's just what you want people to think, isn't it?'

No. He *was* heartless and unapproachable.

Normally.

Normally, when his brain was operating at one hundred per cent capacity. Normally, when he was with any other woman but her. He felt a frisson of unease slither through him as her fingers once again threaded through the hair on his chest.

Now he should get her up. Send her back to her room. Give her every indication of how this situation was going to play out.

Her breathing became choppy and he knew she'd sensed the subtle sense of dread that had overcome him.

'Did I just ruin everything with my big mouth?' She lifted her head, uncertainty threaded through her voice just as her fingers had been lightly threading through the hair on his chest before he'd ruined it.

'No,' he said gruffly. He moved a hand into her hair and gently urged her head back down onto his shoulder. 'Sleep.'

She let out a sigh that whispered across his skin like the sea breeze.

Leave. He'd meant to say *leave*.

CHAPTER ELEVEN

LEXI woke the next morning and the first thing she registered was that she was smiling. The second, as she moved her legs and rolled over, was that her body felt different.

Languid. Replete. Achy.

Her eyes flew to the empty pillow beside her and then around the masculine bedroom. Empty, both. She breathed out and let the sense of happiness glide over her again.

Leo. Last night.

And then another emotion took hold.

Panic. What had she done?

She rolled back onto her stomach and groaned into the pillow. She'd come to his room last night because she'd been worried about his state of mind. She'd stayed because… because…he was just so male. So commanding. When he'd said, 'Come here,' in his rough, accented voice she had felt powerless to resist. Hadn't wanted to resist. Some part of her knowing that to do so was pointless. This thing between them had been building since the moment she'd first walked into her office and seen him standing there like a modern day terminator, about to take her room apart if he didn't get what he wanted.

After her initial uncertainty last night she had felt so uninhibited. So free! Her insides started to melt at just the thought of all the things they had done together.

It was everything she had ever fantasised sex could be and more. So much more. When he had moved over her and his body had first joined with hers something inside her had shifted and she remembered thinking that she would be forever changed after that. That no other man could ever possibly make her feel the way he did.

But that was absurd…and unnecessarily sombre.

Feeling silly at the thought she lay still, straining to hear any signs of life in the outer rooms of Leo's private suite. Almost relieved when she didn't hear anything but seagulls circling overhead and the low, intermittent murmur of distant voices through the open balcony doors.

Relaxing slightly, her mind flashed back to his childhood revelations. She felt warm knowing that he had trusted her with such sensitive information and wondered if he'd told anyone else. He wasn't at all what she had expected after meeting him in her office. He wasn't the privileged, shallow bigot she had first thought.

Like her, he was damaged. He truly believed he had nothing to offer his son but the pain he had experienced as a boy. She thought that if his father was in the room right then she would smack him. How anybody could hit a child she didn't know and her own childhood upset at having an absent father faded into the background compared to the agony Leo had suffered.

Lexi instinctively felt that there was no way Leo was like his father. There was no way a person who hurt others cared about his staff the way Leo did and nor would they care that their son might feel afraid spending a weekend in a strange apartment with a nanny he had never met before. Nor, she felt sure, would they get six monthly checks carried out on a son they supposedly didn't care about to ensure his safety.

Ty!

She'd forgotten all about him!

Was he okay? She knew that he liked Carolina but Carolina wouldn't know where to find her if Ty should need her.

Jumping out of bed, she quickly scrambled around for her dress and felt a blush flood across her cheeks as she remembered that Leo had torn it down the middle.

At least her knickers were still in one piece. She found them on the carpet and wriggled into them, berating her memory for reminding her how he had peeled them slowly down her legs last night. Shaking off the effects of those memories she walked into Leo's wardrobe, her eyes growing bigger than balloons as she took in the rows of beautifully crafted male clothing on offer. All of it formal, or semi-formal. She felt a bit awkward riffling through his shelves in search of a T-shirt and a pang of regret that he had not stayed to wake her this morning punctured the small bubble of bliss she had been feeling.

Last night he had said she was beautiful, feminine—and she had felt as if he adored her. Only that was silly. He didn't adore her. He wasn't even here.

And why wasn't he here? Had last night not been as good for him as it had been for her? She swallowed hard and pushed those unwanted thoughts aside. He was just busy. He had things to do. He wouldn't have had time to wait around for her to wake up and wasn't it more considerate that he'd left her to sleep?

Yes. No. Maybe. It would have been nice to have been kissed awake by him. Had he wanted to do that? Had he even stopped for a moment beside the bed and watched her sleep? No, of course he hadn't and wanting the opposite to be true was a one way ticket to heartache and misery. She knew that better than anyone.

Finally locating maybe the only casual item of clothing in his wardrobe, Lexi donned a long-sleeved black T-shirt that dangled way down over her hands and covered her almost to her knees. Feeling decently covered, she grabbed her sling back heels and rolled her dress into a tight ball. She considered fixing her hair and straightening the bed but thought maybe it was best to get out of there before the maid showed up to make it.

Or, worse—Leo himself. Because she wasn't sure how she was going to face him now. Cool sophisticate who entered into one-night stands whenever the desire took her, or…actually there was no 'or.' The 'or' was a clinging, love-struck fool. She'd played that role once before with Brandon and it hadn't been any fun then either.

Hearing a clamour of raised voices outside, Lexi walked to the floor-to-ceiling windows that faced port-side and realised that they were docked in Athens.

The yacht must have sailed through the night and it was time to go home. In a couple of hours, last night would be nothing but a pleasant memory. She leant her forehead against the cool glass. Why did that thought make her feel so hollow? Surely she wasn't silly enough to want more from a man like Leo Aleksandrov… A man who had turned short term relationships into an art form.

Last night she had said that she didn't live in a fantasy world and she didn't. Not any more. When she was younger she'd always dreamed of her father coming home, of her parents being reunited, and she hadn't realised how affected she was by her father's abandonment. Oh, she knew the thought of finding love made her nervous and she didn't need to see a shrink to tell her that that was because of her father's inconsistent role in her life and Brandon's treachery. But she hadn't realised until last night how much she had shelved the idea of having a family of her own.

She pushed away from the glass, the revelation strangely unsettling.

And really, it was a good thing that Leo hadn't waited

around this morning. This was more honest. This told her exactly where she stood in his life.

Yes, Lexi smiled to herself, it was a very good thing he had left.

She was lying to herself. It wasn't a good thing.

Slowly, over the course of the morning that had now turned into afternoon, Lexi's insecurities had taken such a stranglehold that she felt as if she were choking.

She hadn't expected him to come chasing after her as if she were the love of his life, but nor had she expected to be totally ignored. His continued absence told her more clearly than words that last night had meant nothing to him.

And she didn't want that to make her feel empty. Sad. She didn't want it to make her wonder if she had actually been terrible in bed. She hadn't seized up as she had done with Brandon but…that didn't make her a femme fatale either, did it? She shook her head. Just the thought was laughable.

Home. She needed to go home. Off this yacht and away from Leo so she could lick her wounds in peace and forget that she'd most likely just made a bigger mistake than she had with Brandon.

She watched Ty splashing around in the pool with Carolina and felt anger start to take hold. She didn't know if it was directed more at Leo or herself, and she didn't much care—it just felt a lot better than self-pity.

Leo had to get off this yacht and the sooner the better. He'd woken up with a horrible sense of well-being that had set his heart beating so fast he wouldn't have been surprised if he'd had a heart attack. He'd been wrapped around Lexi Somers as if his life depended on it. Then he'd remembered everything he'd told her the night before and could have cut out his own tongue. Thank God, he'd had meetings to finish up and guests to see off his yacht all morning to keep him busy.

But now that he was alone in his office his mind turned to Amanda Weston and what he was going to do about Ty. He didn't want the responsibility that came with relationships, knew he wouldn't be any good at them. And despite Lexi's assertions last night that he wasn't like his father, he knew he couldn't be a parent to Ty. He controlled his aggression nowadays but that didn't mean he wouldn't hurt Ty one day. And he'd rather die than do that.

Ty deserved more than he could give. He deserved a man who knew how to be a father. A man who knew how to love.

A crisp knock on his office door brought his mind back and he called out, 'Enter,' with a little more relish than he was actually feeling.

Lexi stood framed in the doorway, wearing a white strapless sundress that was partially transparent where the red triangles of her bikini had dampened the fabric. Her glorious sable hair, also damp from the pool, hung down her back and her chin was angled, her eyes glittering bright gold.

'I'm sorry to bother you, but I wanted to know what time we were due to leave for London,' she said, standing before him as if she had a steel pole for a backbone.

No prizes for guessing her mood, he thought, somewhat humourlessly.

He leaned back in his admiral's chair and wondered what had set her off. 'And good morning to you too, angel.'

'Actually, you're a little late with that particular greeting—it's afternoon.'

Ah, so that was it. She was upset because he hadn't seen her all day. Women always wanted the post-sex cuddle and conversation and naturally she wouldn't be any different. But he'd known that and hadn't that been one of the drivers in keeping him so busy all day? That and the fact that she was so damned nice and that last night had been so damned good.

But was that her fault? And was it anything to truly be worried about?

So he had slept with her and it had been possibly the best sex of his life.

Nyevazhno. Unimportant.

That just proved that his instincts were on the money. He'd known sex with her would be dynamite and it was. And that made the fact that he still burned for her completely normal. What man wouldn't want to repeat an experience like that? He felt his body stir predictably as memories of last night sifted into his consciousness.

And it also wasn't her fault that his life had been turned upside down and punishing her for Amanda's deception was not going to accomplish anything.

'I apologise,' he said in a perfunctory fashion that did nothing to lessen the grim set of her pretty mouth.

'For?' She stared down her nose at him and he realised she wasn't going to make this easy. He could hardly blame her. Last night had been beyond sensational and he'd treated her like a one-night stand. Maybe worse.

He spread his hands out over his desk, choosing his words carefully. 'I should have been there when you woke up this morning. In my defence, I wanted to let you sleep and I had guests to see off. Meetings to finish up.'

'I only asked what time we were leaving, Mr Aleksandrov,' she said dismissively. 'I don't need a breakdown of your whole day.'

Mr Aleksandrov? She was seriously peeved and he felt irrationally annoyed with her. What did she think last night had been about, anyway? He'd made no promises to her.

'I've apologised for my behaviour and I'm sorry I hurt you.'

She arched a brow. 'You didn't hurt me, but it's clear you regret last night and I'm happy to forget it as well.'

'I regret a lot of things about last night, angel, but the sex isn't one of them.'

'Well, that's the part I do regret!' she cried and then

clamped her mouth shut as if she'd said too much. Which she had.

He relaxed back in his chair. 'Last night was phenomenal.'

'Whatever.'

'You don't agree?'

'I'd just like to go home.'

Leo tapped his fingers on some papers on his desk. He wasn't used to women wanting to forget a night in his bed. Quite the opposite, in fact. He glanced down at the folder he was absently tapping and noticed it was the prospectus for a hotel in Santorini his investment team were planning to visit at the end of the week. It was old and barely standing but, still, the proprietor would no doubt pretend he had the upper hand. It was the way business was done here.

But why would his busy team need to travel out here when he was already in Greece? It would be no skin off his nose if he detoured to view the property before leaving the country. It would take half a day at the most and would give him more time to figure out what to do about Ty if his security team failed to locate Amanda any time soon.

'That's not possible, *moya milaya*.' She blinked at him, looking as surprised as he felt at coming to such a rushed decision.

'Excuse me?'

Committed, he continued. 'Unfortunately, I have further business to attend to in Greece and have decided to stay on a bit longer.'

'So why do you need me?'

'I would have thought that was obvious.' Let her interpret that as she would.

'Ty has bonded with Carolina and she's great with him.'

'Maybe so,' he said, recognising that what she said was most likely true, but not ready to have her leave him just yet. 'But yesterday when he hurt himself no one could comfort him but you.' She looked frustrated. 'And last night did you not suggest I should stay on?' he reminded her.

'I suggested you take a holiday with Ty. Not work.'

'And so I will.'

He hadn't planned to do that at all but there was a saying in his country: 'One who sits between two chairs may easily fall down.' Once he found Amanda and worked things out with her he'd hand Ty back, but in the meantime maybe it wouldn't hurt to get to know him a little.

An image of Lexi and Ty lying on the carpeted floor of his private library drawing and laughing together the afternoon before came into his mind. At the time he'd been reminded of images of his own dysfunctional childhood but what had stuck the most was that, rather than feeling awash with the cold sweat of fear he'd felt when he'd first seen Ty at the childcare centre, he'd felt something else. Something calmer. And for the first time he hadn't seen Sasha when he had looked at his son.

Yes, maybe it was time to sit on the chair—at least for an hour here and there between work.

'I can't stay. I have to work tomorrow.' Lexi's words sounded loud in the loaded silence and he frowned. What she had to do was to get back into his bed, but right now he didn't think she'd be too amenable to that suggestion.

She couldn't stay. Not when all he wanted was for her to help him out with Ty. Already her heart was racing at the thought of spending more time with Leo, her mind telling her all sorts of fanciful things. That she cared for him—more than cared for him. Which she didn't, of course. She just wasn't the type to have casual sex and her mind automatically wanted to attach meaning to what they'd done last night. It was what had happened with Brandon. Back then she had ignored her instincts that had warned her he was a player and convinced herself she was in love with him. Thankfully, she was mature enough to see the potential for that now, but still…staying in this man's orbit would be like putting Ty in a chocolate shop and telling him he couldn't eat anything.

'Don't you have someone else who can take care of the centre in your absence?' he asked.

'Sure. I'll call up one of my many minions, shall I?' she tried to joke, but it fell flat.

'You must have other staff who can take over in case of emergencies.'

'I do. But this isn't an emergency and I also have a business proposal I need to write.' A proposal she had planned to work on this weekend and hadn't touched!

'A proposal for what?'

Lexi was so tense at being this close to him and not letting on how much he affected her she nearly stormed out. Only he would likely follow and answering him was undoubtedly quicker.

'A new childcare centre Aimee and I want to open.'

'You're expanding?'

His surprise was obvious and she didn't know whether to feel pleased or insulted!

'Not if I don't get the current building problems ironed out.'

He regarded her thoughtfully and the room grew hotter. 'I will help you.'

'What? How?' She shook her head. That was the last thing she had expected him to say.

He looked at her with benign patience. 'Lexi, I run a global company. I think I might be qualified to help you with a business proposal.'

She hadn't thought of that.

'It's what I believe you English call a no-brainer,' he continued. 'You help me, I help you. And it will make up for your refusal to let me pay you for the past three days.'

Lexi mulled this over. She wanted her new childcare centre more than anything else and Leo was supposed to be an incredibly savvy businessman, but…could she really stay on with last night still lying heavily between them? She squirmed a little and told herself if it meant getting her new business up and running, of course she could.

Maybe…

'What time frame are we talking about?' she asked, standing behind the chair facing his desk.

Leo smiled as if she had already agreed and her lips pinched together. 'I don't expect what I need to do to take more than a couple of days.'

'I'll need my proposal completed by Friday,' she told him smartly.

'We'll do it tonight.'

Lexi sucked in a breath. 'And it's just business, right?' The question was out of her mouth before she'd fully thought it through and it landed between them like a dead weight.

His smile hardened. 'Are you asking me or telling me?'

Lexi could feel her heart galloping behind her breastbone and she just hoped he couldn't see it. Because what had happened between them last night—the way he had treated her this morning—made her feel too raw, too vulnerable for her to risk sleeping with him again.

'Telling you.'

He nodded stiffly. 'Then I will, of course, respect your wishes.'

'Thank you.'

'Sudovolstviyem, moya milaya.'

Lexi didn't know what he'd just said and didn't ask for a translation, just watched as he walked out of the room with the lithe grace of a world class athlete and took all the oxygen in the room with him. Then she flopped onto the chair she'd been gripping like a life buoy.

Well, that was easy. But what had she expected? That he would put up an argument? Insist on sleeping with her?

She felt flat and heavy and strangely deflated and yet she should be happy. Leo was taking his responsibilities as a father seriously and he was going to lend her his vast experience in business to help make one of her dreams come true. What more did she want?

CHAPTER TWELVE

'I THOUGHT the plan was for you to look over my proposal.'

Leo looked across at the frosty woman holding onto the railing on the pool deck as if it were the only thing keeping her alive.

'And we will. But first there is a magnificent sunset to enjoy and an even better dinner to eat.'

'I'm not very hungry.'

'You didn't eat lunch.'

'How do you know that?'

'My chef makes it his mission to inspect each plate that is returned. He pays particular attention to the full ones.'

'I wasn't hungry then either.'

'And the sunset?'

'What about it?'

'You haven't disparaged the sunset yet.'

Her lips twitched at his attempt at humour. 'I'm working up to it.'

Leo smiled. After their tense meeting in his office earlier he'd decided there was no way she would be sleeping alone while she was on his yacht but that perhaps he needed to make up for his earlier behaviour and woo her a little. Not that she was making it easy in a fitted blouse and short summer skirt that drew his eyes to her shapely legs and made him want to lay her across the elegantly set table beside the pool and have his wicked way with her. Frankly, polite conversation was the last thing he felt like right now!

'Work up to it while we eat,' he suggested, gesturing for her to take a seat at the table. She eyed it as if it were a guillotine and he hid a smile. She was a definite challenge and one he was surprised to find he didn't mind rising to.

'I think someone must have misinterpreted your intentions when they set this table,' she murmured almost to herself.

Leo glanced at the gleaming silverware, crystal glasses and a centre candle waiting to be lit. It was a romantic setting and just as he'd ordered.

'It's not to your liking?' he asked as he held out her chair.

She sat, but was careful not to brush up against him. 'It's a touch intimate.'

'Not for what I have in mind.'

She met his eyes sharply as he sat down opposite her. 'Which is?'

'Let's eat first. I always find I argue better on a full stomach.'

Lexi laughed despite herself and told her heart to stop its unruly fluttering.

'Would you care for wine tonight?'

She needed something to ward off the charming man opposite her and nodded up at the waiter holding two bottles in his hand.

'Red or white, ma'am?'

'White. Thank you.' She watched as her glass was filled with sparkling wine and realised she was finding excuses not to look at Leo lest he see how affected she was by the sight of him, the golden rays of the dying sun turning him into a bronzed god. His blue eyes were brilliant in his tanned face, his muscular legs accentuated by the low-riding denim jeans, the sexy casual top… Jeans? Since when did he wear jeans? And why, oh, why did he have to look so good in them?

'You're wearing jeans!' She knew she sounded accusing and took a fortifying gulp of wine to hide the gauche comment.

He looked down at himself. 'You don't like them?'

No, she didn't *like* them—she *loved* them.

'You don't normally wear them to a business meeting.'

He smiled. 'How's the wine?'

Lexi recognised that he was changing the topic—again—and noticed his own glass had been taken away.

'You're not drinking?'

'I don't drink alcohol.'

She gazed at him and wondered if he recognised that his decision to abstain from alcohol was just another way he was different from his father and scolded herself for still trying to find things about him she liked.

The waiter returned with a plate of tempting seafood and, despite her misgivings, Lexi found the whole dinner to be sublime. The chef delivered a six course *menu degustation* of light seafood and vegetarian dishes that couldn't help but imbue a sense that all was well with the world.

Lexi flopped back in her chair and eyed the man opposite her in the flickering candlelight, the quiet evening only broken periodically by the slap of a fish as it broke the surface of the sea, and the soft lilt of jazz music that played through the yacht's complex sound system.

Leo seemed relaxed as well and surprisingly the conversation had flowed easily. He'd told her a little about his travels and his business and had asked her plenty about her own, getting her to explain some of her ideas about where she wanted her business to go. She'd felt a little self-conscious at first but he'd proven an avid listener and was one of the few people whose eyes didn't glaze over when she went on and on and on about her passion. Whenever she was out with Aimee and this happened her friend would slice her hand dramatically across her throat to let her know when she was boring the pants off her listener.

'I don't think I told you that you look extremely beautiful tonight. I like your hair down.'

Lexi's heart lurched in her chest and she told herself to calm down. He was paying her a compliment, nothing more.

She stared at him and did her best to feel composed but he was like a sublime male animal relaxed back in his chair, his eyes intent on her face, making her think about how he had looked as he'd risen above her last night and entered her body. How he had felt in her hand. Big…almost impossibly big.

'Nothing to say, angel, *moy*?'

My angel, he said. But she wasn't his and never would be and maybe that tiny hint of wishing it otherwise meant that she'd had just a little too much wine.

'Maybe—' she cleared her throat '—we should just get on and look at my proposal.' She made to get up and collect her laptop from the sofa she had dropped it onto when she'd first come out on deck but he waylaid her with his hand on her forearm.

Lexi stilled as his thumb brushed across the underside of her wrist, tingling sensations causing goose bumps to rise up on her skin and a shiver to ripple all the way down her spine.

'What's the rush?'

The rush was that she was becoming seduced by the balmy night, the candlelit table, the soft music, the wine, the man… Oh, boy, the man!

'Come. Dance with me.'

'Leo, I can't do this.'

'Sure you can. You stand in the circle of my arms, put your hand in mine, and then you let me lead.'

He smiled wolfishly and she gave a short laugh. 'Very funny.'

He stood up and came around the table towards her. 'Let me show you.'

He grabbed her hand and pulled her to her feet. 'Leo, don't. I can't think straight when you touch me.'

His smile was one of pure male satisfaction. 'You know the secret to a man's heart.'

'I don't think it's your heart that's affected by that comment.'

His arm came around to the small of her back and he started moving her in time with the music. 'Maybe not my heart, but another major organ is definitely involved.'

'Only a man considers his *ego* a major organ,' she said loftily.

He laughed and Lexi felt as if some foreign being had invaded her body and switched off her brain. What was she doing flirting with him like this? He didn't want her. And, even if he did, could she sleep with him again without being swamped by her insecurities? And did she want to? No…

'Leo, please…don't play games with me.'

His eyes narrowed and she looked away. 'Someone hurt you. Someone other than your father.' His quiet concern made her stumble and he gathered her even closer against him, her heart pounding out a litany that was totally out of time with the music.

She felt ridiculously safe in his arms—which was like saying a bunny was safe with a wolf—but did she feel safe enough to talk about Brandon?

She hesitated and remembered all that he had told her the night before. 'I was younger and he was immature—I was too, I guess. We met at university, in the library, and he was persistent. It wasn't till later that I found out a couple of his friends had made a bet that he couldn't get me into bed… We were intimate a couple of times but…sex has never been my forte and he soon found someone else.'

Someone else to take her place before he'd even told her their time together was over!

Leo swore. 'He was your first lover.'

Brandon had been her *only* lover besides him. Not that she was going to tell him that.

'Lexi?' He stopped moving and took her chin between his finger and thumb and forced her eyes to his. 'He was your only lover.' The statement was made with quiet conviction and she cringed.

Oh, God, was it so obvious? 'I never knew nights on the Aegean could be so balmy,' she announced cheerfully as she tried to pull her chin away to look out over the sea.

He tightened his grip, his eyes boring into hers. 'He made you feel inadequate?'

Finally the man asked a question. And if she could be more embarrassed she didn't know how. 'Can we *please* talk about something else?'

'Lexi, you are the most beautiful, sensual woman I've known and last night was…' He hesitated. '*Moy bohze*, I get hard just thinking about last night.' He swore softly. 'I get hard just *thinking* about *you*!'

Lexi was shocked by the vehemence in his tone. 'Is that unusual?'

Leo groaned. 'Angel, that's unheard of for me. But I can see you're having trouble believing that and I'm sorry for my contribution in making you feel that way. Whatever that jerk said to you, I can guarantee he was speaking of his own inadequacies, not yours. This morning I was an ass and… Angel, you take my breath away. I thought that was obvious.'

His voice resounded with raw emotion and Lexi felt years of angst and uncertainty fade into the atmosphere. 'Not to me,' she said huskily.

Leo made a growling sound low in his throat and a thrill of excitement shot through her blood. 'Then it's time I did something about that.'

He drew her slowly back into his arms and tilted her chin up so that she was looking at him. 'I want to make love with you, Lexi. I want to pleasure you and banish whatever negative memories your first lover erroneously planted in your beautiful head once and for all.' He swallowed heavily. 'Tell me you want that too.'

Lexi's breath caught and she stared at him. Emotions bubbled up inside her and her mouth went dry. How did someone resist an invitation like that, knowing what was likely to happen next?

They couldn't.

At least she couldn't. Maybe it was time to stop thinking so hard about the future and to just live in the present. She knew he still had secrets but she wasn't looking to marry the guy. This was just…well, she didn't know what this was other than another night in the arms of a man who made her feel fantastic about herself.

Banishing her doubts and deciding to take a chance, she raised her eyes to his. 'Yes.'

He expelled a rough breath as she placed her hand in his and let him lead her to the corner of the deck to a white sofa, wide enough to encompass ten people with room to spare. He moved back from her and leaned against the side of the boat, his arms folded across his chest, his eyes enigmatic in the light cast by the moon and a few well-spaced down lights. 'Take off your blouse.'

Lexi stood before him and let out a ragged breath of her own, self-doubt tightening her throat. But then she saw the fierce hunger shining in his eyes and it just seemed to melt away. It was time to reclaim her femininity and she realised that was what Leo was helping her to do.

And rather than feeling inadequate, she felt excited. Sensual. Thrilled.

Lexi stepped back and held Leo's gaze as her fumbling fingers worked the buttons down the centre of her blouse. When she was done, she slowly shrugged out of it and goose bumps rose up over her skin as Leo's gaze dropped to her breasts. The night was cool, but she knew her nipples were pointed because of the way this man was looking at her more than the temperature of the air.

'Now the bra.' His voice was thick and as slumberous as his eyelids.

Lexi reached behind her and unhooked her bra. She crossed one arm over her breasts and let one strap fall to her elbows and then the other before cupping her hands over both breasts, feeling even more empowered as she saw his nostrils flare. She held her hands in front of her like some practised courtesan and his eyes cut to hers. 'Drop it.' She held her breath and did as he asked, not sure what to do with her hands as he stared at her.

So maybe not such a great courtesan after all...

He was so still as he looked his fill of her it was almost unnatural and, as if she'd done this a thousand times before, she arched her torso slightly in his direction in silent supplication. Last night she had worried that he would find her too small, now she felt as if she was without equal.

His eyes dropped to her legs. 'Lose the skirt.'

Lexi's lower body flooded with warmth at his rough command. She didn't know how it was that he turned her on so completely but her body was ready for his, even though he hadn't touched her yet—this striptease seducing her as much as it was him. Feeling sexually charged, she ignored her skirt and bent forward instead, hooking her fingers around the edge of her black silk knickers and, making sure that her skirt didn't ride up, she let them slide to the floor. Then she slowly straightened, running her hands up her legs as she did so. Enjoying the way his breath hitched at her provocative movements.

She tilted her face up and studied the fierce intensity lighting his eyes, which looked almost black in the dim light. She didn't think she'd ever wanted anything more than she wanted to make love with this man right now and she stepped forward into his personal space.

'Your turn.'

She watched him take a deep shuddering breath and then he ripped his beautiful top up over his head, one of the seams tearing loudly in the still night.

'You really need to have more respect for clothing,' Lexi teased, releasing a shuddering breath as his hot hands reached out and spanned her waist. He tugged her forward one more step until there was barely a breath separating them and then his eyes connected with hers. 'I'm not in the mood to be gentle.'

She trembled and her own hands rose to spread out over his impressive pectoral muscles, her gaze drinking in the bronzed perfection of his chest and the sexy line of fuzz that bisected his abdomen. 'Neither am I,' she said on a rushed breath.

Her words seemed to release him from some dream state because he groaned and pulled her roughly in to him, her breasts scraping pleasurably against the hair on his chest as he lifted her to his mouth. She let out a long, low sound as he found her peaked nipple and suckled her firmly, her arms winding around his neck to clasp his head.

'Put your legs around my waist,' he growled against her aching flesh.

She did as he asked and Leo bunched her short skirt higher, his fingers digging into the soft globes of her bottom. She was the most exciting woman he had ever known and he couldn't get enough of her.

He delved into her wet heat and he nearly came apart in his jeans as she writhed against him and opened readily to his intimate touch.

'*Bohze*, Lexi, you're so wet.'

'For you. Only for you,' she murmured against the side of his neck.

Groaning, he laid her on the soft sofa behind them with one hand and released the zip on his jeans with the other. She clung to him, her hands on his face, in his hair, her voice one soft continuous moan against his lips. He positioned himself at her entrance and was about to surge deep when her hands stopped their urgent exploration and he felt her stiffen.

'Leo. Protection.' Her voice was a breathless whisper close to his ear and it took him a moment to focus enough to digest what she had said.

Then he cursed. 'Damn. Are you on the Pill?'

She shook her head and a lick of unease spiked in his brain when he realised just how close he was to losing control. He never trusted women with contraception.

Cursing again, he fumbled around in the sagging back pocket of his jeans for the condom he'd put there for just this purpose.

'Hurry up, it's getting cold down here.'

Leo smiled down at her. 'Now we wouldn't want that happening, would we?' He sheathed himself and shifted between her splayed thighs and leaned over her. 'Lie back,' he ordered gruffly, running his hands over her creamy torso and tweaking her nipples as she reclined fully, her dark hair rippling on the pale cushions.

Leo held her gaze as he moved into position and then, unable to extend the anticipation any longer he pushed into her in one slow, powerful thrust.

She made a low keening sound and closed her eyes and so did he. She felt like heaven. Her body so tight. So slick. So soft.

'Leo, oh, God.' Her torso arched off the sofa as he plunged in and out and set up a fierce rhythm.

He felt his climax building too quickly and tried to contain it but for once he couldn't. The erotic image of Lexi splayed out before him, her breathy moans of pleasure…

'Lexi.' It felt as if her name was wrenched from some place deep inside him. 'Come for me, angel, I can't…' He grimaced, sweat beading his brow as he concentrated on giving her pleasure and, just when he thought he couldn't hold back any longer, he felt the telltale contractions as her orgasm hit and he let go in a rush, throwing his head back and practically baying to the moon in ecstasy.

It took forever to come back to earth and steady his heartbeat, the aftershocks of what they'd shared weakening his whole body till he could barely lift himself off her.

He rose up onto his elbow and looked down at her, spread out under him, sated, replete and as comatose as he felt, and he felt his chest constrict. Unnamed emotions rolled through him, seeking purchase, and he buried his face in the side of her neck, not wanting her to see just how much their lovemaking had affected him. Like last time, the instinct to flee gripped him and then her soft hands drifted over the sweat cooling on his back and he felt instantly calm. 'I think I like it rough,' she murmured, planting soft kisses along his hairline.

Bohze, she slayed him. He slid his hands along the length of her torso until he reached her chin and then he turned her face towards his so that his mouth could capture hers. It was a sweet kiss, almost tender after the wild sex. She wrapped her arms around his neck with such gleeful abandon he felt the knot in his chest tighten and chose to ignore it. For tonight, anyway.

'Still cold, angel *moy*?'

'Mmm…cold? I feel like I just flew into the sun.'

'The feeling is mutual, I assure you.'

He moved off her, dealt with the condom and pulled his jeans up to cover himself before scooping her up into his arms.

'Where are we going?'

'My bed. That was just the first course.'

'Well, if you're half as good as your chef, I can't wait for the next five.'

'You realise you just signed the man's termination papers,' he muttered half seriously.

She punched his arm lightly. 'I did not.'

Leo very nearly stumbled; it felt so nice to actually have someone play with him like this and he realised that he felt happy. The only times he'd ever felt like this had been during those rare times when his mother had been happy and Sasha had been alive.

He knew Lexi Somers was dangerous. Unfortunately, she was also addictive and he was nowhere near finished with her yet.

But after a week he would be. He didn't doubt that for a second.

CHAPTER THIRTEEN

'STOP hovering. Go join Ty in the pool.'

Lexi released her tense shoulders and scowled down at Leo's bent head, which was still damp from where he'd been playing with Ty in the water earlier. 'You've been looking at the proposal for half an hour. Haven't you finished yet?'

'You're going to dent my ego, angel, if you think I can re-write a whole business proposal in half an hour.'

Lexi's face fell and she tried not to cringe. 'Is it that bad?'

'Relax. It's not bad at all. In fact, if you should ever find yourself out of a job I'd hire you in a heartbeat.'

'Really?'

'I don't say things I don't mean. From what I can see you've done your homework and there's a definite need in the market. But explain this.' He pointed to a row of figures in a graph. 'It looks like you're charging less than your current business, which seems fine while you build up your clientele, but it never evens out. Even taking into account the different demographic of the new centre, it seems low.'

'The people using the childcare centre can't really afford to pay more and there's a lack of government funding in that zone, which would normally subsidise our income and which we're hoping will change some way down the track.'

'You can't run a business on hope and if you're not careful you'll have to prop up this centre with your first, which will jeopardise both.'

'I know, but if we put our prices up it defeats the purpose of what we're offering.'

'Can you cut back on staff?'

Lexi shook her head. 'I won't compromise quality of care for economic gain.'

Leo sighed. 'I always knew you were a soft touch—I just didn't realise how soft.'

Lexi glanced over at Ty and Carolina, splashing each other in the pool. They had all been playing similarly an hour earlier and Lexi's heart still felt light at the memory of Leo interacting with his son. He still hadn't told Ty he was his father and Lexi wondered when he intended to do that, but she had no doubt he would. Not that she should be thinking about that when she should be focused on work.

'Is it so hopeless, then?' she said, turning her mind back to business and trying to keep the despondency out of her voice.

Leo glanced at her, his eyes lingering on her mouth for so long she thought he might kiss her and her body started to tingle. Last night had been even more phenomenal than the first and now, even when she thought of Brandon, she couldn't conjure up one ounce of insecurity.

'You keep looking at me like that, I'll drag you back to my lair and not let you out all day,' he growled softly.

Her look at *him*!

Lexi's eyes lifted from his mouth and the world receded. Then Ty squealed and the world returned with a thud.

'Right.' He cleared his throat. 'Pull up a seat. You need a contingency plan.'

Lexi sat down and for the next hour became more and more overawed as he took her through one cost-saving idea after another.

'Wow, I'm impressed. If I was a bank, I'd lend you a million dollars.'

His smile was wolfish. 'How do you think I bought my first scaffolding company?'

'Why scaffolding?'

'Honestly, I wanted to avenge my uncle by closing down the company that had been responsible for his senseless death. Then one night, after I got into yet another fight I was sitting in the hospital waiting room nursing a broken nose when the richest man in Russia came on the news. There was something about the way he stood and the way others treated him… I wanted to be him. So I changed tack. Bought the company, sacked the incompetent management team and the rest, as they say, is history.'

'How old were you?'

'Eighteen.'

'Eighteen!' She frowned. 'So you never went to university either?'

Leo looked up from the laptop and realised what he'd just said. He couldn't remember ever suffering from a loose tongue before but, ever since he'd told her his 'charming' childhood story, he could feel that he had become less guarded around her. Which wasn't great because he didn't want to slip up and tell her about Sasha and the selfish part he had played in his death.

He thought about the email from Amanda and wondered why it no longer angered him as much as it had last night. The circumstances were still the same and yet he felt different. Tossing the ball with Ty and Lexi in the pool this morning hadn't been as hard as he had thought it would be. In fact it hadn't been a hardship at all.

Lexi's conviction that he wasn't like his father—that he had a choice—played over in his head. Was she right? Logically it made sense, and he certainly didn't *feel* like he could physically hurt Ty, but could he take that risk and look after him full time on his own? No. It was too great a responsibility and if he got it wrong—the outcome could be fatal.

With past memories forcibly tamping down on his previous enjoyment of working alongside Lexi, he closed the lid of her laptop.

'No,' he said curtly. 'And now I have a hotel to view on Santorini.' He stood up. 'I think you'll find what we did this morning helpful.'

He was about to walk off when he made the mistake of glancing down at her. She wasn't looking at him but he could see that his churlishness had hurt her and something twisted in his gut. It was because of last night. It was because some bastard had hurt her and he didn't want to add to the damage he had done to her self-confidence. In fact last night he'd gone out of his way to make her feel cherished. Hardly a hardship, given how turned on she made him feel. But she also made him feel other things he'd rather not name, let alone face.

'Why don't you come with me?' The words were out of his mouth before he'd fully formed the thought and she looked at him with surprise.

'Seriously?' The smile she shot at him was beyond beautiful.

'I don't see why not. It's a tourist destination. You've never been. You can look around while I work.' He made it sound like a no-brainer but he was questioning his own sanity in making the offer.

'Okay. Great.'

'Meet me at the tender in twenty minutes,' he said sharply.

Fifteen minutes later, Leo marched towards the lower deck, snapping instructions into his phone, and stopped dead as he saw Ty bouncing up and down on the white leather seat of the tender. His eyes flew to Lexi's and he blanked out his moment of disquiet. When he'd extended the invitation he had meant it to be just for her.

'I hope it's okay if Ty comes along,' she said.

'Of course.' He inclined his head, remembering at the last minute that his agreement was to spend time with his son.

But he'd already put in an hour today.

The skin on his forehead pulled tight. If he wasn't careful he'd be spending every minute of every day with both of them. And why didn't that thought fill him with as much dread as it would have a week ago?

'No. Absolutely not.'

'But why not?' Lexi persisted. 'You've finished looking at the hotel and the beach is straight down that path. Have you ever been to a black sand beach?'

'No, and I don't want to.'

Lexi put her hands on her hips and stared straight into Leo's aviator glasses. She knew he didn't want to go to the beach and she hadn't missed the look on his face when he'd approached the tender earlier and spotted Ty seated beside her. She knew he didn't really want him here either but he'd made a promise to her yesterday that he would spend time with his son and she didn't want to think that his promises were as hollow as her father's.

Leo's phone rang and he turned away to answer it and Lexi rolled her eyes.

'Look, Lexi—horsies.'

Lexi followed Ty's line of vision to a row of sturdy grey donkeys, resplendent in their multicoloured rugs and faded leather saddlery. Ty started towards them and Lexi grabbed his hand.

'They're donkeys, sweets, and we can't go that way. Have a look at these colourful rocks instead.'

She didn't think he was going to cooperate but then he acquiesced and moved towards the various-sized volcanic rocks lining the ancient path. She watched him squat down on the side of the path and saw one of Leo's security team move into place nearby. The four men who seemed to follow Leo everywhere were so discreet she actually forgot they were even there.

Lexi cast her eyes around the arid landscape that was so unlike anything she had ever seen before. Tiny cobbled streets full of chatty tourists, incredibly beautiful views of a pristine blue sea from the various rocky outcrops and the quaint white cubed buildings, some with brilliant blue trim, tripping down the cliff faces.

But, as riveting as the scenery was Lexi still found her eyes drawn to Leo in his familiar crisp white shirt and suit trousers. Her eyes stripped away those clothes and she could so easily picture his wide shoulders and lean torso, his long, muscular legs. She knew he swam as a form of exercise but the cut of his body also came from centuries of strong alpha males who had fought the land, and each other, for their very survival.

To stop herself staring at him like an adoring fan she walked to the edge of the path and glanced down the winding red-dirt track to the beach below. It would be a shame to come all this way and not see the black sand but—

'Ten minutes.'

'Sorry?' Lexi turned as Leo came up behind her.

'Ten minutes and not a minute longer.'

Lexi beamed a smile at him when she realised he was relenting about going to the beach. 'And, angel, don't make me regret it.' The words were gruff, but a smile tugged at the corners of his mouth and she felt gloriously happy.

'Okay. But can we ride the donkey down?'

He shook his head as if she were a lost cause and set off down the path.

As they breasted the row of little donkeys Ty's face lit up and she saw a resigned expression flicker across Leo's. When he stopped to converse with the elderly white-haired guide with a bandanna tied around his neck and a blue beret shielding his head she hid her smile beneath the wide brim of her own hat.

She watched as he picked Ty up and perched him atop

his chosen steed and felt as light as a bubble as he then proceeded to walk protectively beside him as the donkey set off at a snail's pace down the hill.

He might not realise it, but he was slowly starting to build a connection with Ty and, once he did, she felt sure he wouldn't be able to help falling in love with him. In fact, she sensed that he already was. The only thing she was really having trouble sensing was what was happening between the two of them.

She knew why she had slept with him last night of course. She had felt emboldened by his obvious desire for her and empowered by her renewed sense of self. He had made her feel sexy. Sensual. And it was proving a hard thing to give up, even though she knew he wasn't interested in anything permanent. But that was okay, she reminded herself. Hadn't she decided last night to stop worrying so much about the future and just live in the here and now?

And the here and now was scorching. Both the sun above her straw hat and the man walking alongside a donkey with his son balanced precariously on top.

To stop herself daydreaming, she let her eyes wander to the family of four ahead. The husband had his arm slung over his wife's shoulders while their two girls giggled exuberantly and clung to their donkeys, the leather saddles creaking at each ungainly step the donkeys took.

The couple looked so relaxed and happy—comfortable in each other's space—that it pierced Lexi to the core. This was what she had wanted for her own parents.

This was what she wanted for herself.

She glanced at Leo and realised he was watching the family as well. Then he turned, his eyes snagging with hers. Lexi felt as if she had her heart in her mouth and forced a nonchalant smile to her lips.

Yes, she might want this for herself one day but she wasn't

silly enough to think she would get it with him even if she wished it otherwise.

So much for not daydreaming.

Surprisingly, Leo found he was enjoying himself. He had walked the stinking donkey all the way down the hillside and was now standing on the pebbled black beach holding a fistful of colourful shells and rocks that Lexi and Ty had insisted on collecting along the shoreline. Lexi had rolled up her lightweight trousers, which clung like a second skin to her sexy bottom, and was holding Ty's hand as the waves gently lapped at her ankles.

He thought of the couple he had seen walking their two girls on donkeys ahead of Ty's and brooded. For a minute he had wanted to sling his arm over Lexi's shoulders and draw her close but her cool smile told him he would be way off base in doing so and it had brought him to his senses. He might be still flummoxed with what it was about this woman that attracted him so much but he wasn't going to be an idiot about it. And while he'd presumed that the attraction would start to wane after he'd had her, it was still early days yet. Give him a week with her in his bed and he'd see things differently.

'Take your shoes off and come in,' Lexi called out to him from the shoreline. 'The water is amazingly warm and silky.'

Like her skin.

'No.' He cleared his throat. 'I'm good.'

The bright smile she'd worn ever since he'd given in and agreed to take them to the beach dimmed a little and he felt like the world's biggest spoilsport. He could enjoy a beach as much as the next person, damn it.

With that in mind, he pulled out his phone and called the tender to come and pick them up directly from the beach. If she wanted to enjoy a beach he'd take her to a real one that wasn't crowded with noisy holidaymakers like this one.

* * *

Lexi closed her eyes and turned her face up to the sun and let another fistful of sugar-soft sand sift through her fingers as she lay on the beach chair Leo had organised to be delivered from the nearby yacht. The beach was privately owned and, since they were the only ones on it, it almost felt as if they were shipwrecked. Shipwrecked with an icebox full of treats and drinks, a beach umbrella to ward off the sun's rays, since there were no actual trees on the island to speak of, and a mega-yacht anchored a little way out at sea with every conceivable luxury known to mankind. She smiled and nearly pinched herself to make sure she wasn't dreaming.

The only sound around her was the sound of Ty and Leo building a sandcastle by the water's edge and the whisper of the gentle waves as they rolled on and off the beach.

This was so far removed from her real life it was like entering a fantastic dream. She just had to keep reminding herself of that every time her mind started trying to build its own sandcastles in the air!

'So what do you think of *this* beach?' Leo's deep voice rumbled from somewhere overhead and interrupted her happy thoughts.

Lexi squinted up at his dark outline and smiled. 'It's okay if you like this sort of thing,' she mused as if she wasn't sure if she did.

His eyes trailed over her and her nipples peaked. 'It seems to me this is exactly the sort of thing you like.'

'Well, the sand is very soft.'

'And hot. Like you. And now me.'

'You could always take a dip in the ocean to cool off.'

'I do plan to take a dip,' he said suggestively, 'but it's not in the ocean. Have you had enough of this beach for one day?'

Lexi felt a zing of excitement deep inside her as his brilliant blue eyes lingered on her lips. She had now. 'Yes. You?'

'No need to ask, angel.'

Leo quickly organised the tender to head over and pick

them up and, after a shower and a light dinner, Lexi returned to her room and wrapped herself in an oversized cotton cardigan before wandering outside to her private balcony. She had thought about heading up onto one of the main decks for a relaxing drink but she was tired from all the sun and lack of sleep the night before, and didn't want to appear as if she was deliberately seeking Leo out. Their relationship had shifted gear in a big way today and she didn't know what to make of it or how to ask what he was thinking without appearing needy and insecure.

She knew he still had secrets and she didn't feel as if she could truly let herself relax with him until she found out more about him. She was desperate to know who Sasha was for one, and why Leo's dreams were so tormented. She'd been wrong about how he felt about Amanda and she didn't want to make up stories in her head about Sasha either, but that seemed impossible for her *not* to do.

'Is Ty asleep?'

Lexi felt Leo's presence just before he spoke and looked over her shoulder, her heart skipping a beat at the sight of him, fresh from the shower in T-shirt and jeans. There was something about seeing him in casual gear that reached out to her. He looked like someone who was accessible and not the out of reach Russian oligarch that he really was. 'Yes. He went out like a light half an hour ago.'

She turned back to stare out over the water and felt him come up behind her. 'And you? How are you feeling?'

Confused.

'Tired. It was a wonderful day. Thank you for taking us.'

He reached out and wrapped his arms around her waist, pulling her back into his chest. 'The day's not over yet,' he murmured against the top of her head.

Lexi let herself lean her full weight into him and soaked up his manly smell, which now seemed so familiar to her.

Gathering her courage in hand, she decided she had nothing to lose by asking the question uppermost in her mind. 'Can I ask you something?'

'You know that always makes a man want to say no.'

'Who's Sasha?'

He stiffened for a moment before fanning his hands out over her belly and bending his knees a little so he could nuzzle the side of her neck. 'Sasha is no one you need to worry about.'

Lexi felt *herself* stiffen this time and gripped the wooden railing more tightly. 'You're not still seeing her, are you?'

He stopped nuzzling her and spun her abruptly towards him, grasping her chin between his thumb and finger and forcing her eyes to his, his expression fierce. 'I'm not your father or your ex, Lexi. I don't play around on a woman if I'm sleeping with her.'

Lexi swallowed, not doubting him for a second but remembering an earlier comment he had made about not having girlfriends, only bed partners. 'That's good to know.'

'Anything else?' His voice was clipped and her heart sank a little when she realised that he wasn't going to answer her question.

'You won't tell me, will you?'

He let out an exasperated breath and released her chin. 'Sasha is not relevant to you and me.'

No, whoever Sasha was, she was relevant to him, otherwise he wouldn't mind talking about her.

Lexi folded her arms and looked down at the tiny space between their bodies. She felt raw and exposed and she could feel the tension coming off him in waves. She glanced up at him and almost raised her hand to smooth the frown line marring his perfect brow. 'And what *is* you and me, Leo?' she asked the other question that had been milling around the outskirts of her mind all day, holding her breath as she waited for his answer, remembering too late her new-found intent to live in the moment.

He rubbed the back of his neck in that telltale sign that said he was stressed. Lexi wondered if her question was the death knell of whatever it was that was going on between them, the thought making her stomach clench painfully.

'I don't know.' He reached out and his hands curved around her hips, the familiar warmth of his touch flooding her lower body. 'But I want you more than I've ever wanted any other woman. Is that enough for you?'

Lexi held her breath. Was it? She knew that if she said no he would walk away from her without a backward glance and deep down in her heart she knew she didn't want that. Not yet. Maybe not ever.

Swallowing hard against that thought, she raised her arms and ran her hands over the taut muscles and sinews of his arms until she reached his shoulders. She felt his body quiver under her touch and heard the whistle of air as he released a pent-up breath between his teeth.

He held himself absolutely still as he waited for her to continue and Lexi made up her mind. She didn't know if his answer *was* enough but she wouldn't worry about the future. And what was there to worry about, anyway, if she made sure her heart stayed clearly out of whatever this thing was between them?

An affair?

A fling?

'I don't know.' She gave him the same answer he had given her because it was the most honest. 'But I know I've never felt like this with any other man and I'm not ready to let it go,' she breathed, raising herself onto her tiptoes and kissing him at the same time as he wrapped his arms around her body and crushed her to him.

CHAPTER FOURTEEN

BUT old habits died hard and three days later, as she sat in Leo's library and hit the send button to email her revamped business proposal to her bank manager, Lexi knew she was getting in too deep.

Apart from one afternoon when Leo had flown to Athens to finalise the business deals that had instigated this trip, he had kept his word and spent almost every minute of each day with her and Ty and it had been lovely. Too lovely. But too often Lexi had caught her runaway heart drumming up stories of a future between them that her practical side had scoffed at.

It was like having a split personality. Or having the puppets Punch and Judy in her head. Punch would start daydreaming and going off on a completely inappropriate tangent and Judy would return and bop him on the head.

Lexi pushed her computer aside and stretched the kinks in her neck and tried to go easy on herself. Because who wouldn't dream of a future with a man like Leo Aleksandrov?

Yes, he was arrogant and demanding and always wanted things his way, but he was also gentle and tender and never ran roughshod over her wishes. In fact, this week, he had almost gone out of his way to *fulfil* her wishes. And not just in the bedroom.

And he had completely eradicated her feelings of insecurity, at least with him. She couldn't imagine ever making love with another man with such joyful abandon and was now gladder than ever that she had been honest with Simon about how she felt. It just pained her that she couldn't be as honest with Leo.

But then how did she feel about him?

She liked him, of course, but…that was all she could ever let it be. Because, as tender as he had been with her, as insatiable as he was in bed, he didn't let himself do emotion. And of course there was still the mysterious Sasha floating around in the background.

'There you are, *moya milaya*.' Lexi looked up, startled by the sound of Leo's voice. 'Come—' he held out his hand to her '—I have a surprise for you.'

'What is it?'

'If I tell you, it won't be a surprise.'

Lexi smiled and pushed her gloomy thoughts aside. They were leaving in two days. Plenty of time to feel gloomy after that. 'Okay.'

He dropped a searing kiss on her lips and almost dragged her out of the library and down to her bedroom. There, in front of her full-length mirror, was a metal rack stacked with what looked like couture evening dresses.

She turned to him, slightly bemused. 'I don't understand.'

'It's very simple. I tore your dress the other night and now I'm replacing it.'

Lexi raised her eyebrows. 'With fifty new ones!'

'You never know when the urge might take me over again,' Leo drawled, the wicked grin on his face sending her pulse rate soaring. 'They are all in your size. Choose one to wear tonight and do what you want with the others.'

Lexi ran her hand over the beautiful gowns. If she sold them she imagined she might just make enough money to pay for the renovations to the building for her new childcare centre! 'This is too much, Leo.'

'Enough.' He waved his hand at her imperiously. 'We

are going to dinner. You have nothing to wear. Ordinarily, I wouldn't mind—but tonight there will be other diners around and I am nothing if not possessive with what is mine.'

Oh, if only she was.

Lexi cleared her throat. 'Where are we going?'

'Get dressed and you will find out. You have half an hour.'

'Half an hour! I'll need longer than that to do one of these dresses justice,' she exclaimed with real panic.

'You do them justice already.'

'Too smooth,' Lexi complained and shooed his grinning face out of the door.

When he closed it behind him she returned her attention to the dresses, not knowing which one to choose.

'Athens! You're taking me to Athens!' Lexi had felt sick the whole time they had been travelling in the helicopter that felt no safer than a tin box being tossed around by one of her toddlers. She had only just now prised her hands from her eyes at Leo's insistence.

Athens spread out below her like a bejewelled cloak, the Parthenon sitting atop it like a porcelain crown.

The helicopter circled lower and Lexi once again covered her face, ignoring Leo's husky chuckle but glad of his strong arm holding her close.

She felt a jolt and then Leo said, 'We're here, angel.'

He unclipped her safety belt as the whine of the rotors ebbed, then jumped down onto the ground and placed his hands around her waist as he lifted her out. 'Lucky you're so small,' he said huskily against her ear. 'Not to mention exquisite in that dress.'

'It's black,' Lexi said almost apologetically, 'but I loved the design.'

'It's beautiful.' Leo looked over her shimmering strapless dress, which fell in elegant waves to her feet with frankly male appreciation. 'I can't wait to tear it off you later on.'

'You will not.'

He laughed at her tone and she knew that if he wanted to tear it off her she could do nothing about it. Then she looked around and realised that they had landed on the top of a building with a clear view of the Parthenon. 'Oh, my...'

'You wanted to see the Acropolis at night. And here it is.'

Lexi swung her gaze back to his and tried not to let every one of her overawed emotions show on her face.

'Thank you. This is the nicest thing anyone has ever done for me.'

He seemed to be caught up by her gratitude and blinked before holding his hand out to her. 'Come. We have a booking in Athens' most revered restaurant and then you can take a tour.'

'Really? We can walk around it?'

'Of course. I didn't bring you all this way just to look at it from afar, angel *moy*.'

Lexi laughed and tried not to be dazzled by his arrogant confidence.

'My mother would love it here,' Lexi mused, gazing around the posh old-world restaurant, with tables set at discreet distances from each other and draped in heavy white linen. 'She's half Greek herself.'

Leo leaned back in his chair. 'That explains the dark hair and golden eyes.'

Lexi laughed. 'My eyes aren't golden; they're a hybrid.'

'Yes. Golden when you're angry and green when you're aroused. They're very alluring.'

The muscles deep within Lexi's pelvis clenched at his intimate tone and she knew from the way his eyes smouldered that he knew it. The man oozed sexuality when he wasn't even trying so when he was... Lexi felt heat sweep into her face and tried to think of something to say.

'I've always hated them. As a child I longed for blue eyes and blonde hair.'

'I love them.'

Okay, not helping.

'We need to change the subject.'

'We need to find a bed, you mean.'

Lexi felt a stupid grin split her face as he reached across the table and took her hand in his, drawing lazy circles around her palm.

'That's not helping either.'

'Have I told you how beautiful you look tonight?'

'Yes. Several times. As are you.'

'Beautiful? Sexy, maybe.'

'And modest.'

'You don't get anywhere being modest, angel.'

Lexi sipped her wine, feeling mellow and content. 'Speaking of getting anywhere, do you think you'll stay in the apartment, or do you think you might get a house with a garden now that Ty is staying with you?'

She'd said the wrong thing. She knew it even before he removed his hand from hers and picked up his water glass.

'Ty lives with Amanda.'

'But Amanda's email…'

'Is rubbish. Once my security team find her I'll sort out the problem and everything will be back to normal.'

Sort out the problem? Lexi felt slightly queasy. He had been *so* different this week. She had been *so* sure…and of course she knew why he thought he couldn't have Ty, but didn't he see he was different from his father? Or was there more to it? Was it that he just didn't want Ty, regardless? A thought Lexi had trouble formulating, let alone verbalising. And why was that? Why did she care so much…?

'You can stop looking at me with those shocked, wide eyes, angel. I know what you're thinking but life isn't a fairy tale.'

'I know that,' she snapped, but she knew part of her wished that it was.

'Then you know that I have to find Amanda.'

Lexi tried not to grimace. 'And if you don't?'

'I will.'

His certainty sent a frisson of dread darting down her spine and she was starting to feel sorry for Amanda. 'Don't be too hard on her, Leo. I think it's possible she suffered from post-natal depression after Ty was born.'

'You feel sorry for her?' His tone was incredulous and she cringed.

'I'm not taking her side, if that's what you mean. I know she tried to trap you into marriage, but I don't see the point in dwelling on that. Life is too short to waste on anger or guilt.'

He stared at her for a heartbeat, his body tense. 'It's also too short to talk about Amanda Weston. Come.' He stood up. 'The Parthenon awaits.'

Lexi was only half paying attention to their personal guide as she wandered through the ancient ruins, her mind on the conversation in the restaurant.

This week she had assumed Leo had changed his mind about Ty but she'd been wrong and it made her feel edgy. She wanted to ask him if he was ever planning to tell Ty that he was his father but the magical night already felt tainted by their earlier discussion and she didn't want to ruin it by getting into another argument. Which was probably very cowardly of her, but she needed more time to digest her feelings before she broached it again.

Thankfully, the flight back to the yacht was a little better than the flight over but that was because she was basically half asleep with her head on Leo's shoulder. Still, if she'd had the energy she would have kissed the deck when the helicopter landed safely on the yacht.

Leo scooped her up into his arms and carried her into his suite. Lexi stood before him, much as she had that first night but instead of ripping her dress in half he gently turned her and lowered the zip at the back. Then he peeled the fabric from her body and proceeded to kiss his way down her spine.

His lovemaking was surprisingly gentle and afterwards Lexi lay in the crook of his shoulder and traced lazy patterns over the hair on his chest. Gradually his breathing eased as he slipped into sleep and, for all her earlier tiredness, she felt suddenly wide-awake.

He had told her a few nights ago that he had never slept as well as he had this week and she was glad. But she was also a fool. What she felt for Leo was ten times—no, a thousand times—deeper than what she had ever felt for Brandon. Because she hadn't really loved Brandon—at least not the way she loved Leo.

She let the words that had been edging into the front of her brain for days now take root and she knew without a shadow of a doubt that they were true.

She stared into the darkened room at nothing in particular and didn't know how she felt about that. Because she didn't know how *he* felt about *her*.

Yes, he'd done nice things for her and, yes, he had spent time with her, laughed with her, helped her whenever she needed it, but was she really any different from any other woman he had spent a week with?

Being on his mega-yacht and sailing around the Cyclades islands was like being in a fairy-tale bubble. In two days she would return to London. Return to work. Return to reality. And she had no idea if he would want to continue seeing her there.

She tried to imagine what it would be like if he did. Movie nights with Todd and Aimee? Dinner in her tiny flat? Or would she always have to go to his penthouse and enter his world? And would she want that?

Oh, it was too hard.

Leo shifted and mumbled in his sleep, his arms tightening and releasing around her. He tried to turn, his brow pleated, and Lexi realised he was starting to have a nightmare again.

She instinctively smoothed her fingers over his forehead, trying to soothe him.

'Sasha?'

The whispered word was barely audible but Lexi heard it. And froze. 'No, it's me, Leo. Lexi.'

He seemed to relax at the sound of her voice and his lips whispered across her temple as he pulled her back down to him, immediately falling into a deep sleep. Unfortunately, it took Lexi a lot longer to do the same.

CHAPTER FIFTEEN

LEXI woke alone the next morning for the first time since they had started sleeping together and knew it didn't bode well.

Then she realised that she wasn't quite alone when she heard Leo talking into his telephone over by the window. He was as naked as the day he was born and the morning sun streaming in highlighted his toned butt and the defined dent where his back muscles met his spine.

She had seen him on the phone many times this week but she had never heard him speaking in such a low personal tone and her stomach clenched, a sixth sense telling her that he was talking to a woman.

Then she remembered how he had called out Sasha's name last night in his sleep. How he had thought *she* was Sasha? Lexi's heart hammered at the thought that he had remembered the dream and called Sasha while she lay sleeping.

Stop, take a breath, she ordered herself. He was not her father and she was not her mother. Hadn't she told him that his parents' story didn't have to be his own? So, ergo, nor did hers!

He switched off the phone and Lexi saw such a distressed look etched into his profile that her breath stalled in her lungs. She didn't want to intrude on what was clearly a private moment for him but nor could she keep quiet.

'Bad news?'

His head swivelled around at the sound of her voice. 'You're awake.'

Her eyebrows rose. 'Yep.'

She was desperate to ask who had been on the phone but he tossed it onto a nearby sofa and turned back to face the window, effectively shutting her out.

Lexi felt her face grow hot and her hands start to tremble at the silent rebuff. For the past few days, whenever the conversation had veered onto the personal he had clammed up and she had let him, not wanting to push him as her mother had pushed her father. But now it was different.

Now her heart was involved and she felt even more vulnerable than before. She remembered her father had had topics that were off-limits and it had meant that at times they had all felt as if they were walking on eggshells around him. Just as she felt she was doing now with Leo.

'Where are you going?' he demanded gruffly.

Lexi stopped at the sound of his voice. She had been so deep in thought she had put on Leo's linen robe and was half-way across the room and hadn't even realised she'd moved.

She hesitated, wishing he would put some clothes on. 'You didn't seem to be in the mood to talk.'

'I'm rarely in the mood for the type of conversation you want to have, angel.'

'A personal one?'

'An interrogation.'

Lexi thought of her parents. Of Brandon. And then an image of the family on Santorini swam into her consciousness. She wasn't silly enough to idealise that they were the perfect couple—everyone had some sort of issue to contend with—but the fact was they *were* a couple. They had *committed* to be together for the long haul. Lexi's father had never married her mother and if she continued sleeping with Leo she would be doing so knowing that the end of their relationship was also marked in the sand.

She thought of the needy, clinging woman her mother had become and Lexi didn't want that for herself. She didn't want to become a victim and right now she felt like both! She liked being in control of her life and falling in love with a man who had no intention of loving her back was certain to erode even the most confident woman's self-esteem.

And maybe it hadn't been the elusive Sasha on the phone. Maybe it had been Amanda. And maybe she could just quit with all the guesswork and ask him.

'I was curious as to who was on the phone,' she defended herself. 'I think that's fairly normal.'

He stared at her for so long Lexi's eyes started to drift down the impressive lines of his taut body, only to snap back up when he said, 'It was my mother.'

'Your mother?'

'She calls this time every year.'

He looked as if he regretted adding that but Lexi was not in the mood to let him off the hook. 'Why?'

His hesitation was fleeting, but Lexi caught it. 'It's my birthday, angel.' His smile didn't meet his eyes and Lexi stared dazedly as he moved towards the bathroom.

His birthday! 'Were you going to tell me?'

And his mother was still alive?

Lexi's mind reeled. His online biography had informed her that his mother had passed away and she'd forgotten it was false. Only half aware of what she was doing, she followed him into the bathroom and saw him shrug as he stopped in front of the mirror. 'I hadn't thought of it.'

'Birthdays are special, Leo.'

'Maybe in your world. In mine they are just another day.'

'I didn't realise your mother was still alive.'

He gazed into her eyes briefly in the mirror before they slid lower down her body, one hand rubbing his jaw. 'I noticed this morning that the inside of your thighs are a little red so I thought I might shave this off.'

Lexi's heart thundered at the image his words brought to mind but she ignored it. 'Do you still see her?'

His eyes narrowed on hers. 'What did I tell you? An interrogation.'

Lexi blew out a breath. He was right. She did want to interrogate him. But that was only because he wouldn't *talk* to her. And if he wasn't going to talk to her, why was she still standing there?

Shaking her head at herself, she walked out of the room, surprised when she heard his voice behind her.

'It's not like you to walk out on an argument, angel.'

She turned, glad that he had slung a towel around his hips. Not that it hid much... She forced her eyes to his and noticed he was looking at the necklace she was fondling. 'I just need some space.'

The scowl on his face deepened. 'Why?'

She threw her hands up in front of her. For an astute man, he could be terribly obtuse at times. 'Because you have things you don't want to discuss and I'm not good with that.'

He paced away from her. 'This is why I don't do relationships.'

'Is that what this is?'

'Obviously not.'

'Leo, people in relationships talk to each other and not just about safe topics. They talk about real issues. Like this. Only you won't discuss anything personal. You didn't even tell me it was your birthday!'

'What the hell is the problem with that? It was the day I was born. Get over it. I have.'

Lexi barely registered the harshness of his tone, still stung by how little she knew about him. And on the one hand that was completely normal. They had known each other for little more than a week. The problem was that if he asked her she would tell him anything and it scared her when he wouldn't do the same for her. 'I guess it just showed me how little of yourself you really share with me,' she said testily.

He shook his head. 'You don't understand.'

'No, you're right, I don't,' she fumed. 'I don't understand why you haven't told Ty you're his father and I don't understand why you won't tell me who Sasha is. You called out her name again last night, just so you know.'

He looked momentarily stunned and she figured that he hadn't remembered the dream after all. 'I've told you Sasha is not important.'

And neither, it seemed, was she.

'If that was really the case then you wouldn't mind talking about her.'

'*Chort vozmi*, Lexi. Sasha is not a woman. Sasha was my brother.'

His brother?

'You have a brother?'

'*Was*. I *had* a brother. He died when he was three.'

Ty's age.

'How old were you?'

He looked distinctly uncomfortable. 'Ten.'

The time he had said his father went to prison. Lexi swallowed, not sure she wanted to find out the two were somehow connected, but unable to stop herself from asking, 'How did he die?'

Leo blew out a frustrated breath and closed his eyes briefly before staring back at her. 'He got in between my parents arguing one day and my father backhanded him into the wall.'

'Oh, my God.' Lexi's hand flew to her mouth.

'I told you there are some secrets you're better off not knowing, angel,' he sneered, walking through the doorway to the sitting room.

His voice was so cold, so clinical, and Lexi knew his brother's death still cut deep. As it would.

She followed and sat on the sofa, her hands cupped between her knees as he made coffee. 'That was why your father went to prison. Why you got into fights,' she said softly. 'I'm so sorry, Leo. You must have been devastated.'

The muscles in his back tensed but he didn't say anything.

'And your poor mother,' Lexi continued, unable to comprehend how bad she would feel in the same situation. 'She must have been so overcome with guilt and grief… Was it any wonder she couldn't look after you properly after an event like that? It would have been so difficult.'

He flicked a switch on the coffee machine and the sound of hot water hissed into the room. Then he turned and pinned her with a hard stare. 'She didn't want to take care of me. But I was glad. I couldn't wait to get away from her either.'

Lexi was shocked by the harsh vehemence of his words. 'Why?'

His eyelids lowered to half-mast. 'You planning to finish this interrogation any time soon, angel? I need a shower. With you in it.'

Lexi stared at him. Was this the best it would be between them? Was this all he had to offer? More secrets?

She thought about her life back in London. Her friendship with Aimee. Her job. Her mother fostering children as a way of giving and receiving love. She felt a million miles from everything right now but *that* was her reality, not *this*. This was a potential fantasy and what had happened to her resolve to never enter into those again…?

Her sigh broke the silence and she stared at a point in the middle distance, despair weighing her down. She heard Leo move and glanced back at him. He was a man in pain and her heart gripped. She couldn't give up on him just yet.

'I realise that this is an intensely painful subject for you, but I think it's eating you alive, Leo. And I think you're still suffering from your mother's abandonment of you at a time when you needed her most.'

'She didn't have a choice.'

'So you keep saying, but...'

'I was responsible for Sasha's death.' The harsh words seemed wrenched from some deeply hidden place inside him.

'What do you mean?'

'I was supposed to be looking after him that night.'

His voice held a wealth of self-recrimination and Lexi's brows pulled together. 'Where were your parents?'

He made a harsh sound. 'Fighting. It was always my job to look after Sasha when they fought. Only that particular night I couldn't be bothered. I was more interested in my computer game than my baby brother.'

He stormed back into the bedroom and Lexi heard the sound of him dressing. His revelation had been shocking and her heart went out to him.

She got up slowly and went to the doorway. He ignored her and continued to button his shirt. 'Leo, you weren't responsible for your brother.'

He continued to ignore her.

'Your parents were wrong to burden you with his safety. You're not to blame for his death. You know that, right?'

When he looked at her his eyes were bleak. 'None of that changes the fact that he's gone. That I let him down. That he would *be* here now if not for me!'

Lexi felt a lump form in her throat at his hoarse tone.

'You didn't—'

'Enough! I've dealt with all this; it's in the past.' He tucked his shirt into his trousers and stalked away from her.

She hesitated briefly before persisting. 'I don't think you have dealt with it.' She eyed him carefully. 'Not if you think Sasha's death was somehow your fault.'

He stopped dressing. 'I was old enough to know better.'

'You were ten!'

He ignored her and Lexi shook her head. Did he seriously believe he should have known better? 'You were only a child yourself. But even if you refuse to see the truth in that, what does it mean? That you have to pay for Sasha's death for the rest of your life?'

He stopped and stared at her and Lexi felt a spurt of hope that he was hearing her. 'You have to forgive yourself, Leo. You have to stop playing God. But you also have to forgive your father. If you don't, you just might become him. A lonely, empty man who was obviously filled with anger and hate.'

His blue eyes were icy as he looked at her. 'Are you done?'

'Leo, Ty needs you. I n—' Lexi stopped on a sudden inhalation. What had she been about to say? That she needed him? No. She didn't *need* him. She *loved* him. There was a difference. One created a dependency, the other a partnership. But he didn't want that and she did. More than ever with him. 'I know you can be a great father to Ty and, no matter what you think, you deserve to be happy.'

'I asked if you were done.'

Lexi wrapped her arms around herself in an attempt to stop herself from going to him. She loved him and he was in pain and she felt it all the way to her bones.

'Leo, I feel sick to think of what you must have gone through as a child, but you don't have to live alone like your uncle, and you would *never* hurt Ty.'

He made a brittle sound in his throat. 'You say that with such confidence, angel.'

Lexi felt him slipping away from her. 'Because you're *different* from your father, Leo. You've already made different choices in your life but for some reason you refuse to see that.' She felt a spurt of anger at his cold detachment, desperate to reach him any way she could. 'You know I'm starting to think you like hanging onto the pain of your childhood. I think it gives you an excuse for never taking a chance on love.'

Lexi wished the words back as soon as they left her mouth because even though she thought they might be true, he most likely didn't need to hear them right now.

Leo turned on her. 'Is that what you imagine is going on

here, Lexi?' he snarled. 'Did you imagine I was falling in love with you? That you had beaten every other woman to the post and would get my ring on your finger?' He laughed harshly as if the idea was ludicrous. 'Because I'll tell you now, I'm not the type to hand out trinkets you can wear around your neck in the hope that one day I'll come back.'

Lexi felt as if she'd been punched. Not only because of what he had said, but also because she could see that she had just done what her mother had done—harangued a man into ending a relationship with her.

But she couldn't be sorry. Not like her mother had been. Because Lexi knew she deserved more from a man. Where her mother would have settled if her father had stayed, Lexi realised that she never would. So, as sick as she felt at losing the man that she loved, she couldn't be sorry that she had forced the confrontation. 'I wasn't talking about you taking a chance on me, Leo,' she said with quiet dignity. 'I was talking about Ty.'

'Leo? Hellooooo?'

Leo blinked at the sound of the cutesy female voice in front of him and landed back at the Duke of Greythorn's swanky London party with a thud.

He glanced down as the blonde curled her fingers around his forearm as she smiled up at him. 'For a minute there I didn't think you'd heard a word I said.'

Leo stared at her. For a minute? Try the last half an hour.

He rubbed the back of his neck and glanced around the opulent hotel room and thought that his investment team had done a good job in procuring it for his portfolio. But that was it. He couldn't care less about the party, or the people in it.

'Look, Sarah—'

'Samantha.'

'Samantha.' He smiled, but it felt like more of a wince. 'To be honest, I didn't. My son is at home with a cold and I'm a little distracted right now.'

'You have a son? Does he look like you?'

Yes. Yes, he did. And Leo felt his heart swell with pride at the fact. He shook his head slowly. 'You know, you're the first person who isn't in his inner circle who knows about him.'

The blonde tilted her head coquettishly. 'I feel privileged.'

Leo frowned. He hadn't told her because he wanted her to feel privileged, he'd told her because for the first time he actually *felt* like it. For the first time he actually *felt* like Ty's father and it pained him to think that Ty still didn't know who he really was.

'Do you have a wife as well?' Samantha purred.

'No.' He shook his head. 'I'm not that lucky.' Lucky? Where had that come from? 'If you'll excuse me, I have to go.'

'Of course. I hope your child feels better soon.'

Leo brooded about the evening he'd had all the way home. It wasn't the party that was the problem, or even most of the people in it. It was him. He'd changed. He wanted more from life than polite chitchat and a fleeting moment of losing himself inside a beautiul woman's body.

He'd only been back from Greece for a week but other than work and Ty, he had to admit that he was bored, and for once he didn't want to just carry on as if everything was okay. Because it wasn't. It was empty.

As if on cue, an image of Lexi's smiling face came to mind and he realised he'd never once been bored in her company. Phenomenally turned on—and exceptionally frustrated—but never bored.

He recalled the moment she had left the yacht exactly seven days ago. He hadn't gone after her straight after she'd walked out of his room, his emotions stripped bare when her pained expression had reminded him of how his mother had often looked at him when he'd disappointed her as a child.

He and his mother had an estranged relationship at best.

He sent her money she didn't use and she called him on his birthday, which made him feel guilty and hurt. The fact was, something had broken between them after she had asked the nursing staff to turn off Sasha's life support system and he didn't know how to get it back.

And Lexi had only exacerbated those feelings with her unrelenting questions that morning. So, instead of going to her straight away to apologise for his callous words, he had done what he always did when emotion threatened to swamp him—he'd switched off. Gone for a swim.

He would have gone to her after he had cooled down but he'd been too late. She had already boarded one of his choppers for Athens—supposedly under his instructions! He'd nearly called it back but he knew how much she hated them and it had been a mark of her desperation to get away from him so he'd decided to let her go. Ty had cried and then become remote. Just like he did when he was trying to stop himself from feeling anything.

'Good evening, Mr Aleksandrov.'

'Good evening, Mrs Parsons.' Leo pasted on a smile and walked through to his sitting room, shrugging out of his dinner jacket. 'How's Ty?'

'Sleeping like a little lamb. I told you the worst of his illness was over.'

'So you did.' He tossed his jacket onto the back of the sofa. 'Do you have that passport yet?'

'Not yet sir, but I'll be sure to tell you when it comes through.'

Leo nodded and walked her to the door once she had collected her bag. 'Goodnight, Mrs Parsons. I'll see you tomorrow afternoon.'

'Actually, I'm back in tomorrow morning, sir. Carolina has an appointment to attend to in the morning.'

'Fine. See you in the morning.'

He saw her out of the door and tugged at his bow tie.

He stopped outside Ty's room and opened the door a whisker to look inside. The room looked vastly different from the way it had before he'd gone to Greece. Gone was the double bed and modern furnishings and in its place was a racing car bed and half a toy store. Leo smiled at the thought of how much he would have loved this room as a child.

All he could see from the dim light given off from Ty's nightlight was a small lump under the covers and a shock of pale hair. He stood beside the bed and watched the steady rhythm of Ty's breathing for some time, automatically smoothing his hair back from his forehead when he stirred.

As if sensing his presence, Ty muttered in his sleep and rolled over. 'Grandma?'

Leo felt gutted as Ty called out for Amanda's deceased mother. How was it that he had got the care of his young son so wrong? How was it that he had been so blind to so many things? Lexi was right, he hadn't faced anything. He'd just buried it in a six-foot pit and piled a heap of manure on top.

He lay down on top of the covers and curled himself around Ty's sleeping body as he had seen Lexi do weeks earlier. A lump formed in his throat and his nose tingled as he fought to hold back tears. This was his son. His own flesh and blood and he'd used every excuse he could come up with to stop himself from feeling anything for him. To stop himself from loving him. And all because he was afraid.

Leo thought about himself as a boy, hiding under his blankets late at night as he listened to his parents fighting and then, full of worry for his mother, creeping into the hallway to make sure she was okay.

He remembered how lonely he had felt, sitting with his back to the wall in a tight huddle. How...stoic. How strong he had decided he needed to be to survive. He hadn't shown emotion even then.

No wonder his mother had said he was like his father! And yet she had still called him every year to maintain a connection with him. Maybe she *had* loved him. Maybe Lexi was right in saying that she had just been so overcome with grief that she had only *seemed* to close off from him. And, drowning in his own grief, he had pushed her away so that he didn't have to face his own guilt. His own fear of hearing how like his father he was.

Leo grimaced. He had unknowingly made himself over in his father's image anyway and he was still doing it.

Bohze; he didn't want that any more. He recalled the blissful nights on the yacht, with Lexi sleeping beside him all soft and warm. He'd convinced himself that it was just sex that had given him the sense of well-being he always experienced in her arms, but it wasn't.

It was her.

He thought again of that last morning they had been together and the moment he'd felt sure she had been about to tell him that she needed him. At the time it had sent him into a flat spin but now…now he was ready to admit that he needed her too. Needed her more than his next breath.

Bohze!

She'd made him care and he'd been so afraid of admitting it, he had driven her away. Had laughed in her face at the notion that he was falling in love with her. Which he was. Had.

He loved her.

The thought hit him with the force of a bullet.

What an ass he was. He loved her and he had pushed her away.

He had to tell her. He had to *have* her. And he was sure she felt the same way. He was sure she wouldn't have given herself to him, lain with him every night in his bed, if she hadn't had strong feelings for him. So okay, maybe not love—*yet*— but he'd move heaven and earth to change that.

'Grandma?'

Ty stirred again and Leo stroked his brow. 'It's not Grandma, Ty. It's Papa.'

He felt a sense of warmth he'd only ever experienced in one other person's arms steal over him and it was as if a lifetime of pain and suffering just melted away. He could feel Sasha in Ty's small body, but it was different.

When he'd held Sasha he'd done so with the arms of a child. Now he could feel Ty with the arms of a man. He could sense his own strength compared to Ty's vulnerability and realised that he didn't feel any of the vindictiveness his father had expressed through violence. He just felt love.

Lexi read and reread the email and knew she should feel happier.

'So Darth Vader has approved the loan?' Aimee said with a gleeful smile as she read over Lexi's shoulder. 'You are such a legend. Three weeks ago, I thought there was no chance we'd get the money but now...' She did a little jig. 'Now we move on to phase two.'

Lexi nodded. 'It's thanks to Leo Aleksandrov that we have the loan approved.'

She flicked through a couple more emails knowing that Aimee was watching her sympathetically. When she had returned from Greece a week ago she had been red-eyed and hadn't been able to hide her misery. Of course she'd told her friend everything. Including the full extent of the hurt Brandon had once caused her, which had been easy because it no longer had any effect on her at all. What hadn't been easy was waking up each morning with the memory of how it had felt to have Leo spooning her, of draping herself over his hard male body, and knowing she'd never experience that again.

'Don't look now,' Aimee whispered, 'but the man in question has just walked in.'

'Mr Hammond?' Lexi looked around despite her friend's warning.

'Not Darth Vader. Leo Aleksandrov.'

'Wha—' Lexi closed her mouth, her eyes fixed on Leo's

blond head as he walked through the main childcare room holding Ty's hand.

'I wondered whether Ty would be back,' Aimee mused. 'Do you want to go out and greet them?'

Did she…?

'No!' Not on your life. 'In fact—' Lexi stood up and looked around for a place to hide '—you go, and lock my door after you. If he asks, and I doubt he will, tell him I'm sick.'

Which she was.

Heartsick.

'Too la— Good morning,' Aimee trilled.

Lexi felt Leo's presence and deliberately kept her eyes on the cooling cup of tea on her desk.

'You must be Aimee.' His deep voice resonated inside every one of Lexi's cells. 'It's nice to meet you properly. I am Leo Aleksandrov.'

'I know.' Aimee sounded breathless and when Lexi looked up it wasn't hard to discern why. Leo filled the doorway of her office, wearing black low-riding jeans and a peacock blue T-shirt that matched his eyes and hugged every one of the hard muscles lining his chest. Wasn't today a work day?

She drew in a slow, discreet breath and tried to put on a brave face. If she had thought about Ty returning to the centre at all she hadn't considered that Leo would be the one to bring him. Amanda maybe, but not Leo.

She looked at him, her brain empty of everything but getting through the next few minutes.

She cleared her throat discreetly before speaking. 'If you want the sign-in sheet, then—'

'I don't want the sign-in sheet.' His dazzling eyes, which seemed impossibly blue, held hers. 'I want you.'

Lexi felt light-headed. *Oh, boy, how easy would it be to misconstrue that statement?*

Aimee made a squeaking noise. 'I think I have some wool

to wind.' She made a dash for the door and Leo stepped into the room to let her past.

Lexi's knees went weak and she dropped back down in her chair, not caring that it made him that much taller.

'So how can I help you?' she asked carefully, pleased with her moderated tone.

'You're wearing more make-up than usual,' he rasped. 'Why?'

Lexi felt herself redden. She was wearing more make-up because she was trying to hide the bags under her eyes from lack of sleep and too many hours pining over him.

'This is what I normally wear,' she lied.

'You don't need it.'

Lexi cleared her throat again. This was excruciating. 'I can't believe you stopped in here to discuss my make-up requirements,' she said, wishing he'd just say what he had to say and leave.

'No.' He rubbed the back of his neck and she noticed for the first time that his own eyes didn't look that rested either. Was Ty keeping him up? He wouldn't have been happy to see her leave the yacht, but he had seemed fine with Carolina…

'I came to tell you that I'm buying a new house.'

'A new house?'

'With a garden.'

'Oh.'

'And a pool.'

She nodded, not trusting herself to speak.

He pulled out the visitors' chair and sat down opposite her, looking far too big for the tiny structure. 'Don't you want to know why?' he asked carefully.

Lexi took a deep breath. 'If you want to tell me.'

'I'm keeping Ty.' His words were quiet and sure, his eyes shining. Then he shook his head. 'That makes him sound like a pet. What I meant to say was that I have agreed to take full custody of Ty and Amanda has agreed to see him during the holiday periods.'

Lexi swallowed and contained the surge in her heart with some difficulty. 'So...' she cleared her throat '...I need to amend his forms.'

'Damn it, Lexi, I don't give a stuff about Ty's forms.' He rose and stood in front of her as if he wasn't sure what to do next and then he paced to the back of the room. '*Bohze*, I'm making a hash of this.'

'Making a hash of what?'

He frowned. 'Of telling you how I feel. It's because I've never done it before.'

Lexi was pleased he wanted to tell her how he felt about Ty, but really she would have felt less pain stretched out on a rack of ten-inch nails with rats gnawing on her stomach.

'Leo, I couldn't be happier for you and Ty but—'

'I'm not here because of Ty. I'm here because of us.'

Lexi watched him warily. 'You made it pretty clear last week that there was no *us*.'

'I said a lot of stupid things that morning. Most of them, as you rightly pointed out, because I couldn't let go of the past. I'm sorry I hurt you. In my defence, I was feeling a little unhinged that morning.'

'Because your mother called?'

'Because my mother called. Because our lovemaking the night before had been so damned beautiful.' He paused, watching her as if trying to gauge her reaction to his words. 'For years I buried myself in work and refused to face Sasha's death because I was afraid to let emotion in. Only you made it impossible for me not to feel. Not to *care*. But the truth is angel...' his voice cracked '...the truth is that I love you.'

'You love me!'

'Not just love you. I adore you. I fell in love with you the minute I saw you and—' he grimaced '—I've been running—' He stopped. Stared at her. 'You took off your necklace.'

Lexi reflexively touched the place her necklace had hung for too many years, her mind still spinning from Leo's passionate declaration. 'It was time.'

'No; I ruined that for you.' His voice was soft, remorseful. 'I'm sorry.'

Lexi shook her head. 'Please don't apologise. I had some growing up to do where my father was concerned. For years I refused to face that he wasn't coming back, idealising him as much as my mother had, but I was living in the past. When I was younger I wore the necklace to keep a connection with him, but over the years it had become a habit. And I guess, as you said, I never wanted to admit that he chose his other family over us.'

Leo obviously heard the catch in her voice because he rounded her desk and pulled her out of her chair and into the warmth of his embrace. Lexi sank against him like a stone, her nostrils flaring as she drank in his familiar male scent. God, she had missed this. Missed him.

His hands ran over her back soothingly.

'Angel, he was a weak man. Like my father. They could never accept responsibility for their actions. I was like that for a time but you pointed out to me that life is a choice. We may have been given a bad start, but if we really want something different we can have it. At least I hope we can.'

She raised her head and dared to hope that maybe his declaration of love before wasn't just a fantasy she had conjured from thin air. 'What do you mean?'

He shook his head and moved back to perch on her desk, taking a deep breath. 'I need to touch you but…' he folded his arms tightly across his chest '…first I need you to know that, even though you refuse to see what I have inside of me, I nearly killed a man once.'

Lexi stilled. 'Tell me.'

'It was a month after my uncle's death. He was in a bar, spouting off about his promotion because of his cost-saving strategy. A cost-saving strategy that meant he'd bought substandard equipment that had ended my uncle's life.' He swallowed and she knew how hard it was for him to talk about this. 'I saw red. Hit him. And I didn't stop. Four men had to pull me off him. If they hadn't…' He shuddered.

'Leo, you were young, hurt. What you did was wrong, but I know that deep down you're not a violent person.'

'I nearly hit Tom Shepherd.'

'But you didn't.'

'Because of you.'

'No. You chose not to. Leo, you might have used your fists when you were younger, but—' she took a chance and stepped forward, cupping his face in her hands '—I know that's not who you are now.'

'Lexi, I love you. Marry me.'

'What? You don't do commitment.'

'That's because I've never been in love before. But I'm not letting you go, *moya milaya*.' His hands dug into her waist and his lips claimed hers in an elemental kiss that went on as long as time. Finally, when breathing once again became a necessity, he released her mouth and leant his forehead against hers. 'I used to think that love was to be avoided at all costs. That it meant nothing but pain. Now I know that one day with you in it is worth a thousand without you. I've missed you, angel. Say you'll marry me. Say you'll make me the happiest man alive and Ty the happiest child by giving him ten siblings.'

Lexi felt so choked she almost couldn't speak. 'Ten!'

'Okay, maybe I'm thinking of the practice more than the reality of ten kids, but at least two. Whatever you want. I will be yours to command for the rest of your life if you'll have me.'

She smiled. 'Really?'

'Yes.' The glint in his eye was devilish. 'Of course you will have to wear a very short skirt when you do it.'

Lexi's insides melted as she recalled their incredible love-making that night on his pool deck.

'I think I can manage that,' she murmured huskily.

'For ever?'

'It will take me that long to believe this is all true.'

'Oh, its true, angel, and I've a mind to show you just how true right here on this desk.'

'Only we're in the childcare centre and that's a really clean window,' she pointed out.

'I told you your standards were too exacting.'

'No, they're not. They've just been holding out for you.'

Leo groaned. 'I adore you Lexi Somers.'

He kissed her fiercely. 'And you haven't said it yet.' His voice had a rough quality that held a note of uncertainty.

Lexi stroked her hands over his chest and reached up to loop them around his neck. 'I love you.'

'And?'

'And yes, of course I'll marry you.'

A slow grin spread across his face. 'That's all I wanted to hear.'

'You're very easy to please.' Lexi laughed, feeling wildly ecstatic at the realisation that the man of her dreams loved her as much as she loved him.

'Actually, I'm not. No woman has ever come close to pleasing me the way you do. You're the most beautiful woman I know—inside and out—and I still don't think I deserve you.'

'You do, Leo. You definitely do.'

'Shall we go and tell Ty the good news?'

Lexi felt her heart swell. It felt as if she had loved Ty since the moment she'd first met him but… 'What if he doesn't accept me in such a permanent role in his life?'

'Lexi, he adores you. As do I. Come. You have nothing to worry about.' He looked at her fiercely. 'Ever again.'

Lexi knew her eyes were glowing with happiness. 'Have I told you that I love you?'

Leo smiled down at her and gathered her in tight. 'Not enough, angel.' He brought his mouth to hers. 'Not nearly enough.'

* * * * *

#3107 A RING TO SECURE HIS HEIR
Lynne Graham
Tycoon Alexius is on a mission to uncover office-cleaner Rosie Gray's secrets, but getting up close and personal has consequences!

#3108 THE RUTHLESS CALEB WILDE
The Wilde Brothers
Sandra Marton
When Caleb Wilde's night of unrivalled passion with Sage Dalton results in an unexpected gift, he stops at nothing to claim it!

#3109 BEHOLDEN TO THE THRONE
Empire of the Sands
Carol Marinelli
Outspoken nanny Amy Bannester may be suitable for Sheikh Emir's bed, but the rules of the crown forbid her to be his bride.

#3110 THE INCORRIGIBLE PLAYBOY
The Legendary Finn Brothers
Emma Darcy
Legendary billionaire Harry Finn is formidable in business and devastating in the bedroom. What he wants, he gets... Top of his list? Secretary Elizabeth Flippence!

#3111 BENEATH THE VEIL OF PARADISE
The Bryants: Powerful & Proud
Kate Hewitt
A passionate affair on a desert island wasn't top of Millie Lang's to-do list; but one look at Chase Bryant has her thinking again!

#3112 AT HIS MAJESTY'S REQUEST
The Call of Duty
Maisey Yates
Will tempting matchmaker Jessica agree to Prince Drakos's request? Share his bed before he takes a *suitable* wife?

You can find more information on upcoming Harlequin®
titles, free excerpts and more at www.Harlequin.com.

HPCNM1212